RAWHIDE JUSTICE

When O'Brien, a handsome young drifter, saves Uriah Cahill from a pack of hungry wolves, Cahill explains that he is on his way to join a buffalo-hunting outfit run by Elias Walcott and persuades O'Brien to come along. But the company's foreman, Cyrus McComb, is unwilling to let anyone stop him winning Walcott's daughter. When it becomes clear to O'Brien that the desirable Molly Walcott has fallen passionately in love with him, he and Cahill decide it's time to move on. Fate, however, has other ideas . . .

RALPH HAYES

RAWHIDE JUSTICE

Complete and Unabridged

LINFORD
Leicester

First published in Great Britain in 2016 by
Robert Hale
an imprint of The Crowood Press
Wiltshire

First Linford Edition
published 2019
by arrangement with
The Crowood Press
Wiltshire

A catalogue record for this book is available
from the British Library.

ISBN 978–1–4448–4075–9

Published by
F. A. Thorpe (Publishing)
Anstey, Leicestershire

Set by Words & Graphics Ltd.
Anstey, Leicestershire
Printed and bound in Great Britain by
T. J. International Ltd., Padstow, Cornwall

This book is printed on acid-free paper

1

At the age of ten Cyrus McComb had set the family dog on a cousin and then calmly watched from a porch chair as the animal mauled the other boy. His other, more regular entertainment was pulling the wings off blue-bottle flies, and poking his father's pigs with a sharp stick from the safety of a barbed-wire fence. More recently, in adulthood, and prior to his joining Ogallala Hide Company as a buffalo hunter, he had become a wanted man in three states and the Indian Territory for robbery, rape and murder. His present employer, Elias Walcott, had no knowledge of this law-flouting background, and had made McComb a foreman over his riflemen.

On a clear crisp April morning, after McComb had been with the hide company for just over a year, the company was out on another hunt. A long line of mounted men sat their nervous mounts at the crest of a hillock that looked down on a long slope to a large herd of 'shaggies' a hundred yards distant. The hunters were downwind of the herd, and the buffalo were not yet aware of their presence. McComb was situated near the centre of the line of horses, and an acquaintance of his named Luis Navarro was on his right. Out in the front line Walcott walked his mount slowly, looking his men over. They bristled with Remington lever action, Henry and Hotchkiss rifles. Behind them, stood several long hide wagons, harnessed to dray horses.

Walcott reined in down the line near McComb and Navarro. 'I've said this many times before. Hunting is the most honourable of professions, and the first one that God ever gave to man. Be proud that you are a part of it.' He moved on his saddle and it squeaked under his weight. Down the line the mount of a man named Spencer whinnied and jerked around for a moment.

'That all-knowing God placed us on this Earth to tame and dominate the lower beasts and make them submit to our own use. That's what we're about here. Your predecessors competed up close with the dread saber tooth and came out victorious as the greatest hunters the world has ever seen. Feel his pleasure in your accepting the mantle of those heavy-browed ancestors who began this holy war against the base creatures that cohabit our world with us.'

Spencer, a thin young man, was busy trying to keep his horse under control. Other horses were also guffering impatiently now. McComb turned to Navarro.

'If that sonofabitch starts quoting scripture, I swear to God I'm going to fire off this rifle and ride on down there by myself.' He was big and thick set, a brawny man with a lantern jaw and hard, piercing eyes.

Navarro grinned. He had fled to Mexico six months ago to avoid arrest by the Federates for a list of serious crimes, and had befriended McComb upon his arrival with the company.

'I will break into his office one day and steal his goddam Bible, you wait and see. He will be yelling about it for a year!' Spencer continued in a thick accent.

McComb looked toward Spencer down the line. 'Looks like Spencer can't handle that mount of his.' He gave a crooked grin.

Navarro nodded. 'Isn't he the *hombre* you warned away from Walcott's daughter?' He knew that both McComb and Spencer had tried courting Walcott's blonde daughter Molly. McComb grunted. 'That little weasel ain't got the chance of a snowball in hell with that girl. She's sweet on old Cyrus here. So I had to enlighten him, that's all.' He leaned over toward Navarro. 'When we get down there in the action, keep an eye

4

out for Spencer. You might find it entertaining.'

Navarro gave him a quizzical look just as Elias Walcott raised his hand high above his head.

'All right gentlemen. Go make some money for the company.' Then his arm came heavily down.

In the next moment all hell broke loose. The long line of riders erupted in a chorus of deafening screams and yells, and spurred their mounts down the slope toward the big herd. Halfway there the buffalo began stampeding away from the danger, but it was much too late. In seconds the riders were galloping in among the herd, rifles barking out as animals began falling all around them. The roaring of the stampede mixed in with that of the riders' horses and the firing of rifles. Men could not hear themselves call out to others, nor the roaring of their rifles firing. Dust swirled into nostrils and eyes as buffalo fell all around the hunters, kicking and grunting in the high grass, making the ground shake when they hit.

In the middle of the mêlée the dun mare of the young fellow Spencer began bucking violently. Before he understood what was happening Spencer was flying through the air with shaggies all around him. Then he hit the ground hard. Within seconds of the fall a big hulking bull thundered past Spencer. One of its hoofs staved in his skull just before another animal ran directly over him, breaking ribs and severing his spine. He was dead within moments of his skull being mashed.

McComb and Navarro were near by, and saw the whole thing. But then they were firing at the last of the herd, following it a short distance down the valley. In a few minutes the firing tapered off and the herd was gone over a distant hill. The valley floor was littered thickly now with big black shapes of shaggies. Riders were slowly returning to a central area where most of the killing had taken place. Elias

6

Walcott was riding among them, congratulating individual hunters.

Navarro spurred his mount over to McComb, staring toward the body of Sam Spencer. A hunter had dismounted and was kneeling over it.

'Did you see that?' Navarro said soberly to McComb.

'I saw it,' McComb said easily, out of breath slightly from the action.

'Is that what you meant,' Navarro added 'when you said to watch him?'

McComb put his finger to his lips. 'Come on, let's take a look.'

They rode over to where the grizzled hunter bent over Spencer. The older man looked up at them and shook his head.

'He's all busted up,' he reported.

'Damn!' McComb snapped out. He and Navarro dismounted and stood over the corpse. 'That boy was going to be as good as they come.' Navarro gave him a narrow look. In the next instant, Walcott rode up.

'McComb! I want you back here

showing them new boys how to get the skinning done.' He looked down at Spencer. 'What the hell happened here?' The hunter that had been kneeling over the young man spoke up.

'He was bucked off his mount, Elias. He's bought the farm.'

'I don't understand it,' McComb was saying soberly. 'Spencer was a damn fine rider. Wasn't he, Navarro?'

Navarro looked quickly from him to Walcott. 'Uh. Yes, *cierto*. One fine *hombre*, boss.'

Walcott dismounted too. 'Well. This is a dangerous occupation, boys. I reckon Spencer knew that.'

A rider came toward them across the open field, leading an unmounted horse. He stopped beside Walcott.

'We corralled Spencer's mount,' the lanky young man said to his boss. 'And I think that we figured out what caused all the trouble.' He handed down a small handful of burrs to Walcott who took them. He stared hard at them.

'You mean you found these . . . ?'

The hunter nodded. 'That was stuck up under the animal's saddle blanket,' the other man said. 'Some low life put them there. Probably as a joke.'

'God in Heaven!' Walcott muttered, staring at the burrs.

'*Jesus y Maria*'! Navarro said under his breath. He glanced at McComb, and McComb gave him a dark warning look. Then he turned to Walcott.

'I swear to God, Elias, I'll look into this. I promise you. And if I find the bastard that did this, he'll wish he never heard of our outfit.'

'I appreciate that, McComb. I can always count on you in matters like this. Now go show them boys how to get a nice clean skin off these beasts. Segar, you and Cheyenne get this body aboard one of the hide wagons. We'll give him a decent burial back in town.'

McComb nodded to Walcott and walked his mount off with Navarro beside him. Navarro looked over at Mccomb as they rode.

'You wanted the girl all to yourself,'

9

he said quietly, referring to Molly Walcott.

McComb met his gaze with a diamond-brittle one. 'You did good back there.'

'How did you manage it? The burrs?'

McComb shrugged. 'I distracted him. Just before we all got ready to go. Told him I was fixing his blanket.' A hard grin. 'The weasel believed me.'

'I am glad I never visited the girl.' Navarro cast him a wry look.

'The dumb kid couldn't really ride, or he wouldn't have fell off his mount,' McComb offered. 'It's his own damn fault. I didn't know he would get his head stove in.'

'But now you have Molly to yourself, yes?'

'Listen. All this that's gone between us.'

'Yes?'

'That don't never go past you and me. You understand me?'

Navarro swallowed when he saw the look in McComb's eyes. 'Of course,

10

compadre. We are *amigos si?*'

McComb did not respond. They had arrived at a group of men who were slicing hide off buffalos with big Bowie knives. McComb reined in.

'Come on, I got to show these new recruits how to skin a shaggy.'

Then they were both dismounting to join the others. A short distance away, Spencer's mount was being led past with its lifeless rider slung over its saddle.

* * *

A little later that same day, about two days' ride from Ogallala, out in the Wyoming Territory, a young man riding an appaloosa stallion reined in at the crest of a low ridge. He leaned forward on his saddle, scanning the terrain ahead. His name was O'Brien, and he was seeking his future in this remote wild country. He reached forward and patted the neck of the stallion.

'I know, it's been a long day. It will be

dusk pretty soon. I think there might be a stream up yonder another hour. We'll make hardship camp there.' He had just purchased the big, brawny horse a week ago in Laramie, and was still getting acquainted with it.

He spurred the gray-mottled mount down a gradual slope onto a broad meadow fringed with cottonwoods. He was a tall wide-shouldered young fellow in his mid-twenties, wearing fringed rawhide tunic and trousers, and a dusty Stetson over long, shoulder-length hair. His eyes were deep piercing blue, and he wore a neat mustache typical of the time. The few women who had encountered him had considered the young man handsome, but with a caveat: he seemed like a man you did not just go up to and introduce yourself without an obvious invitation.

In less than an hour's ride farther in the end of the day, O'Brien crested a knob hill and got his first look at the small stream he knew about from previous travels through this country.

This was where he intended to spend the night. But as the sun set behind him and the sky began to darken he squinted down and saw the camp fire near the creek. A drama seemed to be unfolding there.

A man stood a few feet from his fire with a rifle in hand; he was surrounded by a pack of gray wolves.

'Oh-oh,' the rawhide man grunted in his throat.

A dead wolf lay almost at the man's feet, but two others now charged at him. No snarling, no noise at all. Just deadly business as usual. The man fired the rifle and one of the two was stopped short of him, yelping and twisting as it hit the ground beside him, almost knocking him to the ground. The second animal reached him, and did knock him off his feet. Then two more were on him as he now used the rifle as a club, swinging wildly as they tried to grab at his arms and legs to tear flesh.

O'Brien's appaloosa guffered nervously as its rider quickly dismounted and slid a Winchester 1866 lever-action rifle from its saddle scabbard on the horse's flank. He quickly reached into the ammo belt at his waist and inserted a few more cartridges into the chamber of the long gun. Then he was on one knee, finding the besieged camper in his sights. Light was fading, and O'Brien realized that to save the man's life he had to act fast.

Another wolf now lay stunned beside the man but three were on him, growling now and tearing at his clothing. Fortunately he was wearing a sheepskin jacket and thick trousers.

O'Brien found a big wolf in his sights, one was up near the man's head and neck. The Winchester barked out in the dimming light, and the wolf at the man's throat jumped spasmodically into the air, and fell heavily to the ground, where it lay thrashing about.

The fallen man and the other wolves searched the immediate area with their eyes, but only a couple of the wolves actually saw O'Brien. The ones on the

14

man went back to their attack. O'Brien fired again, and a second animal jumped wildly and fell. Now there was only one wolf on the man, and it now moved away, looking right at O'Brien and his mount. The others did, too.

'Be careful. They see you,' the man called out. O'Brien could see dark patches on his clothing where blood had seeped through.

The words were no sooner out of his mouth than two of the remaining four wolves began a headlong rush at O'Brien. He fired at the first one at fifty yards, and it jerked sideways and fell, shot in the head. By now the second one was thirty yards away and then twenty. O'Brien fired without aiming, and the animal was hit in the chest, exploding its heart. It still came on and almost knocked O'Brien over, he could smell the iron scent of its pelt as it brushed past him. Then it fell dead behind him.

Now a last bold wolf made a desperate charge at him, but was brought down halfway through its rush. It kicked and jerked on the ground for a moment as O'Brien re-sighted on the last one. It looked at O'Brien darkly, making up its mind. It looked down at the fallen man. But when it realized what had happened to its pack, it quickly turned and ran into the nearby woods.

It was over.

The appaloosa guffered and buckled nervously, eyeing the dead wolves all around them.

'I know,' O'Brien told it, touching its muzzle. 'It's all done now.'

A moment later he was aboard again and riding on down to the campsite. The other man had regained his feet.

'You come along at a good time, stranger. I had myself buried with quarters on my eyes.'

O'Brien said nothing. He looked the fellow over, then dismounted and picketed the stallion to a sapling. He walked over to the other man, and examined his clothing and wounds. The man just watched him. He was middle-aged, with a grizzled-gray beard and a long bony face.

'My name is Cahill,' the fellow announced, showing yellow teeth. 'Uriah Cahill.'

'I got some bear grease for them wounds,' O'Brien told him. 'They ain't bad.'

He walked over and threw a chunk of wood on the fire.

Cahill followed him over there, moving his arm and making a face. In the next few minutes O'Brien retrieved a small bag of bear grease from a saddlebag, helped Cahill get his jacket and shirt off, and applied the grease to a couple of deep wounds. When he was done he went and got a pan to fry some rabbit meat in. While he was cooking it over a low fire, Cahill joined him.

'Much obliged, stranger.'

'I got enough rabbit for two.' He poked at the fire.

'I didn't get your name, young man.'

O'Brien turned the dark-blue eyes on

him. The name is O'Brien.'

'You done some fancy shooting there. You a hunter?'

O'Brien poked at the fire. 'You writing a book or something?'

Cahill grinned. 'You don't talk much, do you?'

'When it serves a purpose.' It was dark now, and O'Brien served up some rabbit meat and corn dodgers. Cahill supplied some hot coffee. They ate in silence for a long time. When they were finished, and their implements had been washed with creek water and the appaloosa settled in, they sat together under a starry sky. O'Brien was unwinding from a long day's ride.

'Are you feeling better?' he asked at last.

Cahill nodded. 'I'm fine. I owe you my life, mister.'

O'Brien gave him an acid look. 'Forget it.'

Cahill sighed. 'I'm a simple mountain man. Trapper. But it's all worked out

18

around these parts. Now I got to do something to earn a living. Or starve.' A small smile.

O'Brien looked over at him. He was beginning to like the man. 'I done some trapping myself. Most of it back in the Shenandoah Valley.'

'Oh, you're from the East.'

O'Brien didn't pause to think about it but he felt at ease with this fellow.

Maybe, he thought, it had to do with saving his life.

'Grew up in Virginia. Killed my first bear at eight.' A slight grin. 'Was trading with the Cherokee at ten. It was a hardscrabble life.' He got up from the fire, walked over to a wolf's corpse near by, grabbed it by the tail, and flung it away from the camp. 'I reckon your horse run off.'

'He'll be back by dawn. He's done this before. He don't like wolves and bears. Silly beast. Why did you come out this way.'

'The diphtheria took my family down, and I wanted to start a new life

19

somewhere. Now, can we forget the history lesson?'

Cahill grunted. 'Sorry. Just making palaver.'

O'Brien sat there staring into the fire and thinking. By this time it was all starting to run together in his head. A year before the War between the States was over, when O'Brien was just sixteen, he had wanted to join up with the Confederates, but his immigrant Scots father had told him he would shoot O'Brien in the leg to keep him at home. After his folks and sister were gone and buried, he had taken the Ohio west, and then hired onto a wagon train that was going to Texas. He was a cattle drover for a while there, then began riding shotgun for Wells Fargo. He had been fired from that job just a week ago after he had a dispute with a boss and knocked him down. He had been looking for an area for good trapping when he came upon Cahill.

Cahill poked the fire with a stick and sparks flew up into the blackness.

Out on the prairie somewhere a coyote howled at the moon.

'I was born and raised in Texas,' Cahill said quietly in his soft drawl. 'Never liked it. Rode north to Colorado and started trapping and selling the pelts at the Fort Griffin Rendezvous. Or trading them off to Blackfeet and Crow for food and equipment. I built and abandoned a half-dozen cabins in the mountains. They are still there, probably. When the beaver and ermine played out, I moved on. Now I got other ideas.'

'I been looking for something myself,' O'Brien said. 'Maybe do some cowpunching at one of these big ranches hereabouts.'

Cahill suddenly looked over at him in the firelight. 'Say. That name O'Brien just rung a bell. There was a man by that name that folks call the White Lakota.'

O'Brien stared at the fire. 'Hmmph.'

Cahill grinned. 'That's you, ain't it? By Jesus, that's you!'

21

O'Brien glanced over at him. 'Don't never call me that.'

'How did that come about? The name?'

O'Brien sighed. 'It was when I first come out here. On a cattle drive in Nebraska I went looking for a stray heifer and was dislodged from my mount. Fell hard. My employer never found me. But the Lakota did. Chief Gray Hawk took me in till I was well again. Liked it so much I stayed on for a while. Learned a little of their tongue, and their habits. They'd found me at the mouth of a cave I had drug myself to. The kids of the village thought I lived in the cave.'

Cahill snapped his fingers. 'That's it! They told it around that you emerged from a bear cave full-grown and was put there by the Thunderbird.'

O'Brien shook his head. 'They seem to like stories like that. They also say I can't be killed by a bullet. It's all bull-pucky and peyote smoke.'

'I think I can guess where that come

from. The bullet story. The same Bible drummer that heard the White Lakota story said you attacked a gunslinger in Laramie one night while he emptied his gun at you, and beat him to death with your bare hands.' He glanced over at O'Brien and reassessed the big size of him.

O'Brien frowned at him. It was one thing to save a man from ending up in a wolf's belly, but another to sit through all this.

'Like I said, let's forget the past history.'

'Just one more question. Did that really happen?' Cahill asked tentatively.

O'Brien let a long breath out. 'In the first place, that didn't happen in Laramie. Some liquor-crazy drifter decided to kill me because I didn't laugh at his joke. He didn't care that I wasn't carrying iron. He just started blasting away at me.'

'Good Jesus.'

The fire cracked at their feet. O'Brien threw a small chunk of wood at it and sent more sparks flying.

'He only hit me twice out of five shots, and one hit was just a graze. I went on in and threw a punch that broke his jaw and something in his neck. He hit the floor and never moved again. He still held his gun and its barrel was smoking. But I never beat him to death.'

'No,' Cahill said, giving him a look. 'You did it with one punch.'

O'Brien picked up a stick and studied it. He hadn't talked this much to anybody in the past six months.

'You never know what will happen in a brawl. That lead he put in my ribs was still festering weeks later.'

'You want another cup of coffee?'

'I think I'll pass. Oh, there's your horse.'

Cahill's zebra dun mustang had just meandered into the camp behind Cahill and now it guffered at him. O'Brien's stallion returned the greeting. Cahill rose and went over to the mustang.

'So there you are, you mangy beast! Now that the danger's past it's OK to dally with us that stayed and fought.' He grabbed the horse's reins and took it over to the tree where the appaloosa was tethered. The animals touched muzzles.

'He seems to like your gray,' Cahill said with a smile as he returned to the fire.

'They get along a lot better than people,' O'Brien observed.

Cahill poured himself a cup of coffee and resumed his seat on a thick chunk of wood. O'Brien was sitting on his saddle.

'There's nothing like a set-down in hardship camp,' Cahill remarked, more to himself than O'Brien.

'You must like being alone, though,' O'Brien suggested. 'Trapping by yourself in the mountains.'

'I can handle it either way,' Cahill answered, sipping at the hot coffee.

O'Brien could smell the aroma of it. 'I'd prefer going it alone, I think. I met some damn fools on ranches, and at Wells Fargo.'

Cahill grinned. 'I avoid townsfolk like the plague. They can talk you to death about horses and women.'

They exchanged slow grins and then studied each other's faces for a moment, each realising they had some things in common.

'You ever think of buffalo hunting?' Cahill said after a long moment.

O'Brien shook his head. 'Only been on one hunt. With Chief Gray Hawk. The Lakota won't kill a buff if they can't use the meat as well as the hide.'

'Well, that's different from the way the white folks go about it. You ever run across one of the hide companies?'

O'Brien shook his shaggy head. 'Can't say I have.'

Cahill's narrowed eyes, the colour of granite, glistened in the firelight.

'A couple of days' ride from here, in Ogallala, there's a man I know by the name of Elias Walcott. He owns a hide company over there, and operates all round that area. It's a big business now, because of the new demand for buffalo robes back east.'

'I've heard about them,' O'Brien commented. 'That never appealed to me much.'

'I met Walcott when I come up here from Texas,' Cahill said. 'He owned a ranch near Wichita. I worked for him about a week before I headed for the mountains. He's a Bible-thumper, but not a bad fellow.' He looked over at O'Brien. 'My luck has petered out, trapping. I've decided to head for Ogallala. I heard Walcott was looking for a few more hunters to round out his crew.'

'Sounds like he'd be glad to see you,' O'Brien offered. The fire was guttering out, and he decided to let it die down.

Cahill caught his eye. 'I been thinking about you, young fellow. I reckon you'd do to ride with, and I don't say that about just anybody.'

O'Brien studied his face and said nothing.

'Do you think you might like to try buffalo hunting for a while? If I'm reading you right you ain't got any big plans. And Walcott pays twice as much as you'd get cowpunching.'

O'Brien ran a hand over his dark mustache and his blue eyes went very serious.

'Gray Hawk says the big hide companies are like locusts,' he said. 'They come and feed off the prairie and leave it wasteland.'

'I know their methods are rough-hewn,' Cahill replied, 'and I wouldn't want to make a career with Elias Walcott. I'm talking about getting ourselves a grub-stake there, and then moving on. I think we could both use a little cash for our pokes.' He paused. 'I just picked up a couple of Kansas City newspapers last week. You can find out what's happening in the big world out there when we take a break for the mounts.'

'I don't read or write,' O'Brien said.

Cahill looked over at him soberly. 'Oh.'

'I was only taught shooting, tracking, and preparing meat for the table. There was never any schools near by.'

'Well, out here shooting is a lot more important than reading. And it's just what Walcott needs. I could teach you to read.'

O'Brien scowled at him. 'I don't need no goddam little-boy school lesssons, Cahill.' Then he added menacingly, 'I get along just fine without all that.'

Cahill saw he had gone too far with this young loner, and the tone of O'Brien's voice made his throat constrict.

'Sorry again, O'Brien. Don't pay no mind to me.'

O'Brien looked out into the night. 'I might ride there with you. Just to look the situation over.'

'That's just what I'm doing,' Cahill said, trying a grin. 'I'm glad I'll be riding with you, partner.'

O'Brien gave him a sober look. 'Let's see how it goes.'

2

Cyrus McComb was seated at a long trestle-table in the big mess hall, having his evening meal with the other hide company hunters who had been with him the previous day when Sam Spencer had been killed.

There were several other long tables in the building, and a long counter on one wall where food was served to the workers on tin trays. At the other tables were hide-trimmers, scrapers, tanners and others. The groups usually ate at their own tables and did not mix much. McComb's riflemen were always exclusive in their habits because they considered themselves a cut above the other employees of the company, and to be its backbone.

McComb ate hungrily, glancing at the faces of the men across the table. One of them, an Irishman named

Flannery, looked up at McComb occasionally as he ate, sober-faced. He had not spoken to Elias Walcott, and would not, but he had seen McComb at Spencer's horse just before they all assaulted the herd out there, and had his doubts about what happened.

Luis Navarro, who knew what had caused Spencer's death, sat across the table from McComb and ate his beef stew quietly. He had been with McComb when they all arrived back in town that day, the wagons loaded with 'green' hides, and McComb had repeated his promise to Walcott that he would get to the bottom of the mystery that surrounded Spencer's death. He sat there now eating as hungrily as McComb.

'Cyrus. Did you and Walcott make arrangements for Spencer?' His intention was to give credence to his sidekick's fictitious concern. McComb stopped eating, and spoke very loudly to the table.

'That brave boy will get a fine burial

tomorrow, and Walcott will expect every mother's son of you out there at Boot Hill.' He looked over at the other tables, where everyone knew what had happened and raised his voice: 'And that goes for the rest of you reprobates.'

'Have you found out anything about how it happened yet?' Navarro continued in the same vein. There was just the edge of a smile on his lips after he spoke, unnoticed by any at the table. McComb shot Navarro a quick, dark look.

'I examined the saddle and blanket. I saw the remains of a tumbleweed on the blanket. Maybe he laid it on the ground for a minute when he saddled up here in town and picked up all that stuff. That's what we'll go with now. But if I find out anybody fooled with that gear after he got it on, I'll kill the bastard myself! And that's a by-God promise!'

A rifleman down at the end of the table, across from McComb, spoke up.

'I'm not trying to throw mud on

nobody here. But somebody seen you over at Spencer's mount just before you saddled up to ride, McComb.'

Navarro looked over quickly to McComb. A scowl grew slowly on McComb's square face. There was a thin scar that started on his left jaw and ran down onto his neck, and it turned pink as he rested a deadly gaze on the speaker.

'Is that you, Jenkins? You still eating with your fingers or did somebody give you a fork this time?'

A few men along the table laughed softly. McComb took a breath in and laid his fork down carefully.

'Now just who was it that told you I stopped at Spencer's mount, flea-brain?'

Men stopped eating, even at nearby tables. Jenkins swallowed hard, and glanced at Flannery, two places down from him.

'Come on, boy,' McComb urged ominously. 'Share what you got.'

The Irishman, a recent immigrant,

33

cleared his throat and spoke in a heavy accent.

'Sure and it was me that saw it. I make no accusations here. But as you walked along the back of the line, as you often do, you did seem to dally at Spencer's mount. And your hands was on his gear.'

McComb was about finished with his food. He pushed his tin tray away now and clasped his hands before him. Everybody at the table had stopped eating.

'Flannery, Flannery,' McComb said quietly. The entire mess hall had now gone tombstone silent. Servers behind the long counter had turned to watch the table.

'I'm sure you had your reasons, Mr McComb,' Flannery added.

McComb turned a look on him that turned Flannery pale under it.

'I told Spencer why I stopped there. His blanket was all twisted up at the back because he wasn't careful putting it on. He apologized as I fixed it. And I didn't see no burrs under there because I was only working on the edge of it.' He looked along the line of faces across the table.

'It's just that Flannery thought you was there quite a while,' the fellow Jenkins spoke up again, rather apologetically.

'Let it go,' Navarro called out down the table. 'Are you two loco?'

But McComb was on his feet. His hand went out over the Colt Army .45 he always carried on his hip.

'Get on your feet, you goddam snake!'

All eyes in the big room were all on McComb. Down at the end of the table Jenkins was slack-jawed.

'I was just talking, McComb. I got no fight with you.'

'Maybe you don't hear good,' McComb growled. 'I said get on your feet and back up your words like a man.'

'Hey, slow it down, McComb,' called one of the tanners at another table.

McComb glanced at the man hostilely, then turned back to Jenkins. Jenkins had risen slowly from his seat.

'I ain't going to draw on you, McComb. Me and Flannery ain't making no charge against you. You can rest easy on that score.'

'I don't give that credence,' McComb spat out. 'I bet you been flapping your lips all over this compound. A man has to defend hisself. Go for your iron.'

There was absolute silence in the room. A scraper across the way placed his fork down on his tray and it sounded like a small explosion. Jenkins jumped slightly. McComb had cooled down, though.

'I should shoot you down like the yellow dog you are,' he growled.

'Let it go Cyrus,' Navarro said from across their table. 'He is not worth it.'

McComb slowly relaxed, and his hand moved away from the Colt.

'A saucy manner does not go down

with me,' he said finally, resuming his place at the table. 'Nor wild accusations. They don't set well in my craw.' He forked up some stew. 'Spencer was a friend, and I'll kill any man that calls me a liar.'

'And that goes for both you locos,' Navarro added to him.

Jenkins had quietly sat back down, exchanging a quick, surreptitious look with Flannery. Flannery turned toward McComb.

'We don't want to get crossways of you, boss. You got a perfect explanation for what happened out there. We're flea-brains, both of us. Brash as camp cooks doing brain surgery, and that's the truth of it.'

That lightened the mood in the room, and a few men laughed lightly. McComb ate his stew.

'If any man-jack of you finds any evidence of tampering with Spencer's saddle, you bring it right to me, and I'll take it to Walcott.'

A few men muttered their assent to

the order, and the subject was closed for good.

★ ★ ★

After the evening meal McComb returned to his bunkhouse across the compound. The company complex consisted of several sizeable buildings besides the long mess hall and the kitchen, with three bunkhouses, a main work building where hides were processed, Walcott's office, a warehouse where finished hides were readied for shipment to customers back East, and a recently installed tannery.

When McComb and Navarro were alone in the bunkhouse momentarily, Navarro grinned at McComb.

'You handled that *muy bien* back there, *amigo*. If you had not shown such anger, they might have known you were lying.'

McComb was changing his shirt, putting a clean, cotton one on. He showed a brawny, muscular frame with a second scar along his rib cage, put there in a long-ago knife fight.

'I told you. What I said out there. That never happened. There's no evidence to connect me with any of it.' He gave Navarro a narrowed look. 'And there never will be.'

'Of course not, my friend. Are you going into town?'

McComb grinned. 'Walcott will be in his office here most of the evening. I thought it might be a good time to pay Molly a little visit. When we can be alone for a while.' The grin widened.

Navarro laughed softly. 'Ah. The cause of all this trouble.'

McComb's grin dissolved into a scowl. 'Maybe I didn't make myself clear.'

Navarro raised his hands defensively. 'Yes, yes. *Lo siento.*'

McComb left the building a moment later without speaking further to Navarro. He retrieved his chestnut stallion from the corral behind the buildings, saddled up, and rode on into Ogallaia.

Even though the hide company was located a short distance from town on a small stream called Whiskey Creek, Elias Walcott had chosen to build his two-story Victorian house almost in the centre of Ogallala. Walcott had lost his wife Rebecca a few years back to influenza, and had tried to raise his young daughter Molly by himself. But he had been much too involved with the company to pay much attention to her, and she had grown up 'spoiled rotten', with almost no discipline or guidance.

At eighteen now, she had recently discovered the power of sexual good looks, and was becoming an irrepressible flirt, with company men and those from town alike. At this time, however, Molly was still virginal.

When McComb arrived at the Walcott house, it was dark outside and there was a soft glow of oil lamps coming from the downstairs windows.

McComb tethered his mount to a hitching rail at the street and announced himself at the front door with a loud knocking. After a moment a black maid answered the door, squinting into the dark night.

'Yassir?'

'It's Cyrus McComb, Annie. You going blind on us?' A chuckle sounded in his throat.

Oh, Mr McComb. Mr Walcott, he not here. He at the office.'

'I'm here to see Molly,' McComb said patiently. 'Is she here?'

'Oh, yassir. Step right in, Mr McComb. She upstairs, I get her.'

McComb stepped into a long foyer with an oriental carpet on the floor and potted palms standing in corners. A broad staircase led to the upper floor, and within a short moment of Annie's calling for her Molly Walcott came gliding down the stairs to the foyer.

'Well I declare. If it isn't Daddy's backwoods foreman, Mr McComb.' She was a fairly tall, slim girl who filled

41

out her gingham with pleasant curves. Long, blonde hair hung shoulder-length, and a chiselled face held large blue eyes and a pouty mouth. She flirted at McComb now with those pretty eyes.

'What brings you here on this quiet evening, Cyrus?'

McComb shrugged. In the few times he had visited her he had decided to play her flirty game. If she were not Walcott's daughter he would have forced himself on her when he first saw her.

'I thought we might sit and talk a little, Molly. And who knows what else?' A sly grin accompanied this last remark.

She gave him a sexy smile, then reached and adjusted his shirt collar. In an intimate way. It was the way she flirted with every man who came courting. Molly loved the attention and encouraged it democratically, no matter who the man was.

'There won't be nothing else, silly'

she said in a purring voice. 'Good heavens, you are such an impetuous man.' She took his arm. 'We'll go into the library here, but leave the door open.'

McComb made a face and they went into the private room. McComb had been there before, but was always impressed. Another large oriental carpet covered the floor, there were several pieces of overstuffed furniture placed here and there, and a fireplace contained a low-burning fire. The wall in which that fireplace was set was otherwise filled with bookshelves, from floor to ceiling.

There were history books and biographies, among many others. There was an entire section devoted to various editions and translations of the Holy Bible, and several ancient prayer books.

McComb envied the man who owned all this, and in the back of his mind, he envisioned himself married to Molly and inheriting everything Walcott owned. He had no real feelings for

Molly, except to get her into bed. She was merely a stepping-stone to bigger things.

Molly sat down on a soft chair near the fire and offered a similar one to McComb. McComb had hoped for the long sofa, where they could sit together.

'Are you going to the funeral tomorrow?' she asked innocently. McComb's face clouded over.

'Of course. I'll see you there.'

She looked at the fire. 'I kind of liked Sam. He said the sweetest things to me. Daddy liked him, too.'

McComb stared at his hands. 'It was a damn awful accident.'

'You didn't like him, did you?'

McComb looked up quickly. 'He was alright. A little stupid, maybe.'

'You didn't like him because of me.' A coy smile. 'Admit it. You didn't like it that I saw him occasionally.'

'That boy had clabber for brains, thinking that he had a chance with you.'

'Who says he didn't have a chance? I say anybody has a chance. I like it when men come to call on me. You ought to get used to it, Cyrus.'

McComb rose from his chair, bent over Molly and pulled her to her feet. He grabbed her close to him, and planted a hard, long kiss on her lips. It was the first time he had ever kissed her.

Breathless, blue eyes showing shock, Molly broke from his grasp and slapped him across the face. She had been kissed by boys since she was twelve years old, but had never been kissed by a mature man. It sent unexpected thrills of emotion through her, and she liked it, but she didn't want McComb to know that.

'Damn you!' she gasped. 'Nobody kisses me without an invitation.'

McComb was grinning pleasantly through the slap. 'I knew it. You got some cougar in you, girlie.'

'I want you to leave here right know,' she said, still breathing hard.

'You liked it, didn't you?' He grinned.

45

'Cyrus McComb, I mean it. You should leave before I call Annie in here.'

'If your daddy wasn't Elias Walcott, I'd've had you on your back months ago.'

She blushed under the frank suggestion, but again, part of her liked it.

'If Daddy heard you say that, he'd fire you.'

'Don't be so sure about that,' McComb said easily. 'I'm the best damn foreman he ever hired for this outfit, and he knows it.'

She walked over to the doorway. 'You've had a big evening here, Cyrus. It's time for it to be over.'

McComb grabbed his hat from his chair, and followed her to the door.

'We'll take this up some other time,' he said genially. Then he was gone from the house.

★ ★ ★

The next day, the day of Spencer's funeral, was sunny and warm. The

46

funeral went well, with most of the company attending. Walcott quoted some scripture over the open grave, and Spencer was put under ground by mid-afternoon.

In late afternoon, Uriah Cahill and O'Brien rode into Ogallala, tired and dusty from a two day's ride. Cahill stopped a cowpoke coming out of the Conestoga saloon and inquired where the hide company was located. Then he and O'Brien rode on out there without stopping to rest or eat.

The large compound was surrounded by a wire fence, with a high gate for entry. Passing through it, O'Brien was impressed by the size of the operation. The first building the two men encountered was the main work building, with Walcott's modest office shed adjacent. Near by was the new tannery building.

They dismounted outside, tethered their mounts, and went into the main building. It was a high-ceilinged place, full of work benches where men

47

laboured on the raw hides in various stages of production. Toward the rear of the building racks held hides that were curing.

'Good Jesus!' Cahill muttered. 'I didn't know his operation was this big.'

A scraper came over to them, his apron and arms smeared with dried blood and grease.

'You looking for somebody, boys?'

'We'd like to see Elias Walcott,' Cahill told him. 'We heard he was hiring.'

The fellow looked them over. 'You know how to cure a hide?'

'No, no. We want to hunt the shaggies,' Cahill explained. The man gave him a sour look.

'Oh. You only want the easy work. Go out and shoot a few buff and then laze around the rest of the time counting hides over in the warehouse.'

O'Brien was already wondering if this was right for him. He moved over close to the scraper, and stood three inches above him.

'We asked where we can find Walcott.

You going to tell us?' he demanded in a hard, low voice. The scraper stepped back a half-step before responding.

'Well, sure. If that's what you want. I don't know if he's hiring hunters, though. You'll find him in the office through that side door.'

Cahill grinned slightly and nodded. 'Much obliged.'

The small office was just a corrugated-iron shed next door. Walcott was inside, at a scarred desk. A clerk with a green visor and sleeve garters sat at a smaller desk. Walcott looked up when he heard the two men enter.

He stared at Cahill for a moment, then a wide grin took hold of his face.

'My God! Uriah Cahill.' He rose and came over to Cahill, and they clasped hands for a moment, staring into each other's eyes. 'What the hell are you doing here in Nebraska, you old horny toad!'

Cahill was grinning broadly. 'I'm

looking for work, Elias. Me and my friend here. This is O'Brien. He's been working for Wells Fargo.'

Walcott grabbed O'Brien's hand, and then was sorry he had done so. He winced under O'Brien's iron grip and then looked him over.

'My pleasure, O'Brien. You look very fit to work.'

'I done some of everything,' O'Brien said quietly.

'We came to hunt the shaggies,' Cahill quickly put in. 'We can both shoot. And we got good mounts under us. O'Brien just saved my life with his rifle.'

O'Brien gave him a warning look and Cahill changed the subject. 'We just rode two days from the Wyoming territory.'

But Walcott was assessing the tall young man a second time. 'Well. We could use a couple more hunters. We just lost one a couple days ago. Got trampled by a herd.' He smiled at Cahill. 'Still interested?'

'We sure are,' Cahill answered for them both, looking toward O'Brien.

The clerk had quietly left, and now McComb entered the office. He glanced briefly at the two newcomers, then spoke to Walcott.

'We got two hundred hides ready to ship off to Boston. That batch for New York needed some extra currying to look good.'

Walcott nodded. 'OK, McComb. These boys here are looking for work as hunters. An old friend Cahill, and this young fellow calls hisself O'Brien.'

McComb turned to them sober-faced. 'Oh. New recruits.'

'This is my foreman on our hunts,' Walcott told them. 'Cyrus McComb.'

McComb was looking them over. He stared a long moment at O'Brien, who stood almost two inches taller than him. McComb didn't like it if he had to look up physically to any man. He frowned slightly.

'Where you from, boy?' he asked O'Brien.

O'Brien disliked his looks. 'All over,' he said curtly.

McComb wasn't pleased with his reply, or the manner in which it was delivered.

'We wear plain old work clothes around here. Did you come dressed for a tribal dance or something, with the rawhides?'

O'Brien narrowed his eyes on McComb. 'It's what I always wear. They was made for me by the Lakota a while back.'

'I know mountain men that wear them,' Cahill intervened. McComb didn't respond or even look at him.

'Well, we can get you some work clothes if you're hired. So we can tell you from the hostiles.'

Cahill looked quickly at O'Brien to see his reaction.

'I don't wear nothing but this,' O'Brien said. McComb took a deep breath in.

'I see. So you want to be different from the rest of us. A man apart.'

'That ain't it,' O'Brien said stiffly. He turned to Cahill. 'Maybe this ain't for me,' he said. 'I'll wait outside for you, Cahill.'

'No, wait,' Walcott spoke up quickly. He glanced at McComb. 'We don't care what you wear, O'Brien, as long as you can kill buffalo. Ain't that right, McComb?'

They all looked at McComb. He just stood there looking sombre. He didn't like Walcott undercutting his authority.

'Can he kill buffalo?' he said gruffly. 'Wearing that thick ammo belt don't tell me nothing.'

'I saw him shoot,' Cahill said. 'I can vouch for him.'

'Hell, I already decided to hire both of them, McComb,' Walcott said. 'Cahill and me go back a long way, and I've seen him shoot.'

'Well, then we'll just have to look at O'Brien here,' McComb said deliberately. He caught Walcott's eyes with a hard look. 'Like we do with most recruits. I got my crew to protect. That suit you all right, Elias?'

'Well, if you think it's necessary.' Walcott shrugged. 'You don't mind doing a little shooting for us tomorrow, do you, O'Brien?'

'It's your show,' O'Brien told him.

'We'll go out to the range tomorrow morning,' McComb said. 'You can shoot against me.' A small smile played over his lips. He was considered the best shot in the company.

'He don't have to be as good as you, McComb,' Walcott said.

McComb grinned. 'That goes without saying.'

Cahill and O'Brien got a good night's sleep that night in the bunkhouse reserved for the hunters. Several riflemen came up and introduced themselves to the newcomers; one of them knew O'Brien's name. McComb came in late and there was no further exchange with him that night.

The next morning was another bright and sunny day. Walcott, McComb,

Cahill and O'Brien walked out to the rifle range adjacent to the corral, and Walcott put a hide man on paper-on-straw targets a hundred yards distant. Walcott sat on a hard chair while the others stood. McComb and O'Brien went to a firing line on a slab of concrete, while Cahill stood beside Walcott.

'Now, Rawhide,' McComb said to O'Brien, 'let's see if you can hit one of them bales out there.' He turned and grinned at Walcott. Cahill had a slight smile on his face.

The target man signalled he was ready. McComb was holding his Henry 1860 repeating rifle and O'Brien had brought the Winchester from his mount's irons.

'You do much shooting for Wells Fargo?' McComb said.

'Not much,' O'Brien replied.

'You making excuses in advance boy? Your partner says you're pretty good. You can't carry water on both shoulders.'

'Why don't we let the shooting speak for itself?' O'Brien suggested.

'That's just what I figured,' McComb snapped. 'Shall I start?'

'Suit yourself.'

McComb assumed a shooting stance, raised the Henry, and squeezed off three fast shots in a row, the long gun barking out raucously in the morning quiet. At the target, a marker went up and showed two bullseye hits just off centre, and a third just outside the bullseye. Behind the two men, Walcott applauded the performance.

'Good shooting, McComb.' He turned to Cahill. 'That's why he's my foreman out there.'

'Just routine, Elias.' McComb grinned smugly. 'OK, Lakota man. Give it your best try. You don't have to be embarrassed if you can't mirror what you just saw.'

O'Brien made no comment, and faced the target area. He raised the Winchester to his shoulder and the long gun cracked out loudly in the cool morning air. He fired three times, just as McComb had. A moment later the target man stepped out from behind the bale.

'There's only one hole here, bigger than the others. I think he put three in the same hole. Dead centre.'

There was total silence for a moment as that news was absorbed. Cahill was grinning widely. At last Walcott spoke.

'Good Jesus! I never seen nothing like that. Ever.'

McComb stood beside O'Brien, dark-visaged. He stared over at him for a moment, then strode out to the target area. When he got there he examined the target carefully. Then he threw it onto the ground.

'He don't like to be beat,' Walcott confided to Cahill.

In a moment McComb was back at the firing line. He came up to O'Brien.

'I bet you couldn't do that again in fifty tries.'

'Try me,' O'Brien said levelly to him.

McComb held his frustration in. He turned to Walcott.

'Well, it looks like he can hit a standing target. Let's see how he does if it's moving.' He turned back to O'Brien. 'Watch this and learn.' He reached into his pocket, got a silver dollar out, and showed it to O'Brien. 'See if you can do this, Rawhide.'

He shouldered the Henry rifle again, and threw the coin into the air, down the range ten yards. The rifle roared again. The coin jerked in mid-air, then hit the ground thirty yards away. When McComb retrieved it it had a hole in it, slightly off-centre. He grinned at O'Brien.

'Match that.'

'Jesus,' Cahill mumbled from behind them.

O'Brien reached into a poke on his belt and pulled out two coins. Then he went over to Cahill.

'You got any?' he asked.

Cahill came up with two more. Three of the four coins were half-dollars and one was a quarter. O'Brien returned to the firing line.

'What the hell are you up to?' McComb growled at him.

'Shooting,' O'Brien responded.

In the next moment, he hurled all four coins high into the air. Then the Winchester banged out four fast shots as the coins began falling earthward. One by one they jerked as they were hit, and then lay scattered on the ground. O'Brien went to pick them all up. He brought them back and laid his palm open to show McComb. Three of the four had been centrally hit, the quarter had had a chunk taken out of its edge.

Walcott and Cahill hurried over there to see for themselves.

'My God!' Walcott murmured.

'Sorry about the quarter,' O'Brien said 'It was hid behind another coin for a second there.'

Walcott grinned. 'Is he good enough for you, McComb?'

'I wish I'd seen them coins before he

throwed them,' McComb grumbled.

'But he can obviously shoot. If you want him, you got him.' Then he turned without any word to O'Brien, and headed back to the office building by himself. Walcott smiled at O'Brien.

'He'll get over it.' He reached his hand out to him. 'Nice to have you aboard, O'Brien.'

O'Brien took his hand and bruised it for the second time. 'I reckon that remains to be seen,' he offered.

3

The Conestoga saloon was one of three in Ogallala, but it was the finest, and the most patronized by townsfolk, ranch hands and hide men alike. It had a genuine tin ceiling, a large original painting by Remington behind the bar depicting a running horseback fight between unidentified Plains Indians and the US Cavalry, and plenty of sawdust on the floor to absorb the odours of beer, whiskey and sweat.

On O'Brien and Cahill's second evening with the hide company the two decided to ride into town for a couple of drinks before retiring to the bunk-house for the night. When they got to town they were surprised to see it bustling with activity. The saloons and two stores were open for business, their whale-oil lamps brightening their interiors and also the street. A couple of cowboys were racing up and down the main street, firing their six-shooters, and the sound of tinny music came from the Conestoga.

They stopped in front of that saloon and looked around. Neither man had ever been in Ogallala before except to ride through.

'Looks like a Dodge City,' Cahill commented. His middle-aged, weathered face was clean-shaven now, and he had lost some of the tired look he had shown on arrival at the company.

O'Brien grunted. 'Nothing is like Dodge City.' He gave a small grin.

'Let's go get ourselves something to quench our thirst,' Cahill suggested.

A few minutes later they pushed through swinging slatted doors and looked around. The place was ear-rending with boisterous noise that drowned out the piano at the rear. Most of the customers were cowpokes from nearby ranches, and they were the loudest. Most tables were already taken, and the long bar on their left was crowded with men, red-eyed and half-drunk.

There was one table unoccupied not far from the door. The twosome walked over and settled themselves there. Only after getting seated did they notice McComb and Navarro at the next table. They were with two other riflemen from the hide company.

'Hey, look who decided to join the party!' McComb called out. 'Our new recruits.'

'McComb,' Cahill responded quietly.

It did not escape McComb's notice that O'Brien hadn't returned the greeting. His face sobered.

'Look, boys this is the rawhide man that throws shot coins into the air to look good with his rifle.' He laughed gutturally, and Navarro joined in. The other two hunters just stared over at O'Brien.

'There wasn't nothing wrong with them coins,' Cahill said. 'Two of them come out of my pocket.'

McComb shook his head. 'OK, OK.

Have it your way. What you drinking tonight, boys? Sarsaparilla?'

'Let it go, Cyrus,' the Mexican said. 'It spoils the tequila.'

McComb arched his brow. 'My ale tastes the same. I'm having a real good time.'

But two of the cowboys at the bar had heard his accusation about sarsaparilla. They turned towards the tables, shot glasses in hand.

'Look, we got some of them buffalo men in here tonight, Ben. Drinking sarsaparilla like a bunch of New Orleans dandies.'

'They don't smell like dandies.' The other cowboy, Ben, grinned. 'I wondered what that stink was in here. I reckon they can't get all that buffalo dung washed off.'

McComb sighed, his attention taken off O'Brien. It was always this way in town when the cowpokes got their pay. There was always some interplay between company men and ranch hands.

'The stink come in with you cow-floppers,' McComb called back as he swigged down some dark ale.

'Go poke some doggies in the ass,' Navarro shouted merrily, and laughed as he held a glass up in the air.

'Ah! And we hear from the wetbacks too.' The first cowboy grinned. 'Do you miss bedding with your sister, Mex?'

The smile faded off Navarro's face, and he started to come off his seat. McComb put a hand on his shoulder and stopped him.

'Remember, *amigo*, Walcott fires us if we get into it with ranches.'

'What's the matter, greaser?' Ben now said loudly. 'You allergic to gringos?'

Now most men at the bar were listening to the exchange, as were several tables of cowboys and towns-folk. The piano had stopped playing.

'Maybe we better just get on back to the compound.' One of the two hunters at McComb's table said quietly. 'If we shoot one of these jackasses Walcott will fire all of us. He knows all the ranchers around here.'

McComb was dark-visaged. 'It might be worth it to blow a hole through one of these morons.' He was armed, as was every patron in the room except for O'Brien, who never carried a sidearm. He had begun taking his Winchester with him into cafés and saloons in strange towns on the Wells Fargo trail, but figured there was little likelihood of real trouble in this company-dominated town, so he'd left it back at the compound.

Now a third cowpoke at the bar spoke up. 'Who let them hide boys in here, anyway. Can't a man have a drink without the stink of buffalo in his nose? It's goddam disgusting!'

There was laughter around the room. Tonight there were no other hide men in the room but the ones at McComb's and O'Brien's tables.

'By God, I don't think we have to put up with it,' Ben blustered. 'What do you think, Luke?'

The taller man who had started the whole thing nodded. 'I think you're right, by Jesus.' He looked at Navarro. 'Why don't you get your greasy ass out of our saloon, wetback, and take your stinking friends with you?'

'Boy, your head is empty as last year's bird's nest,' McComb growled at him.

'And now, maybe we'll see who leaves here.'

McComb was about to rise off his chair, when he glanced over and saw O'Brien already on his feet.

Suddenly every eye in the room was fastened on the man in rawhides, including those of the troublemakers at the bar. O'Brien picked up a bottle of planters' rye that had been delivered to his table, and took a long swig of it as everybody watched. Then, without setting the bottle back down, he walked over to the bar with it in his right hand. He came up to the fellow called Luke without speaking.

'What do you want, buckskin? You

ain't even armed. You come to smoke a peace pipe?'

To general loud laughter, O'Brien swung the bottle at Luke's head. It smashed into his left ear and knocked him violently back against the bar. He hung there for a moment, looking glassy-eyed, then slid to the floor at O'Brien's feet. Busted glass and spilled whiskey lay all over him and the floor.

There was loud murmuring from the room. Ben, his eyes wide, hissed out harshly, 'You sonofabitch!' Then he drew a revolver on his hip. Before he could pull the trigger, though, O'Brien grabbed his gunhand and shoved it away from him. The gun went off with an ear-splitting roar. Hot lead, missing a bartender's head by inches, crashed into an oil lamp in a distant corner. Then O'Brien started squeezing down on Ben's gunhand, inexorably, like a bear trap.

Ben began yelling as the fingers in his gunhand began to fracture under the iron grip. When the grip was released his gun clattered to the floor. Ben fell moaning against the bar. O'Brien back-handed him with a violent slap that broke two teeth out as the cowpoke joined his cohort on the floor.

O'Brien looked down the bar. 'Anybody else got something smart to say?'

There was a long silence. Then O'Brien walked back to his table, to a grinning Uriah Cahill. He dropped two coins onto the table.

'You ready to get out of here? It ain't quiet enough tonight for my taste.'

McComb and the others at his table were just staring at him.

'Yeah, let's go get some rest,' Cahill said, still grinning.

When they were gone a general murmuring of hushed exclamations filled the room.

'Did you see that?'

'He was one of them hide men.'

'I never seen the like. Not here in Ogallala.'

'Walcott got hisself something there.'

By the time the wonderment tapered

off McComb was twisted up inside with envy.

'I guess we have a tough *hombre* there, heh, *amigo*?' Navarro offered.

'Why? Because he knocked a couple drunks down?'

'Oh. Well, any of us could have done that, *por supuesto*. They were just a couple of *borrachos, si*?'

McComb cracked the knuckles on his right hand with his left. 'Somebody has to take that boy down a notch or two.'

Navarro leaned toward him. 'Maybe a little something under his saddle, heh, Cyrus? Like, you know.' He was momentarily forgetting McComb's warning to him. McComb turned to him with a look that made Navarro's mouth go paper-dry.

'Mex, if your brains was dynamite, you couldn't blow the top of your head off. If I ever hear that pass your lips again, I'm going to blast your liver out past your backbone.'

Navarro found it difficult to speak.

'Excuse, *compadre*. The liquor has climbed into my head. Never again, *lo prometo*. My lips are sealed.'

'I'm heading back to Whiskey Creek.' McComb rose from the table. 'Take my mount back. I'm going to walk it. I need the exercise.'

Navarro nodded subserviently. 'No trouble, Cyrus. Get some fresh air.'

Outside on the street Navarro mounted his own horse and rode off toward company HQ with McComb's stallion trailing behind on a tether. McComb walked on down the street leisurely, trying to put O'Brien and Navarro out of his head. When he reached a residential area not far from the business section, he found himself passing by Elias Walcott's Victorian mansion. Molly Walcott called out to him from a porch swing.

'Good evening, Cyrus,' came the feminine voice from the porch. 'Been having a literary seminar at the Conestoga?'

McComb squinted to see better, and

71

spotted a man sitting beside her on the porch swing.

'I'll be damned,' he muttered to himself. He pushed through a small gate and climbed the steps to the porch.

'Molly,' he said deliberately. 'Dawkins.' Her companion was one of his riflemen.

A young, sinewy Dawkins, about O'Brien's age, grinned awkwardly at McComb.

Everybody knew McComb was interested in the owner's daughter.

'Evening, boss. Ain't it a fine night out here?'

'I been thinking the same thing,' McComb said tightly. 'What are you doing in town, Dawkins? You got a big day ahead of you tomorrow.'

Dawkins was embarrassed. 'Oh, it's early, Cyrus. We was looking at the moon.'

McComb nodded. 'The moon. Well, I want to see you bushy-tailed tomorrow morning, mister, so I want you to go get some sleep. Now.'

'Hey! We were enjoying ourselves here, Cyrus,' Molly protested.

Dawkins rose off the swing. 'It's OK, Molly. We'll set some other time.'

'You just pay attention to your work,' McComb said pointedly.

'Yes sir,' Dawkins nodded. McComb was a decade older than he, and his boss. 'Enjoy the night, Molly,' he added. Then he left. McComb sat down beside Molly. She moved away from him, frowning.

'You quit scaring my beaux away, Cyrus, or I'll quit seeing you entirely.' Her blonde hair was put up behind her head and she looked particularly pretty in the moonlight.

'I told you,' McComb said, 'I don't want you setting with every hide man or cowpoke that comes past here. It ain't fitting for a business owner's daughter.'

Molly laughed a soft laugh. 'You don't want? Who are you to tell me who to see? I'm not promised to anybody, Cyrus. I can do just what I want.'

McComb turned to her. 'You got the reputation for being the biggest flirt in Ogallala, Molly. There are other girls that won't even see you 'cause you ain't fit to set with. I heard it in the store last week.'

Her face crimsoned. 'Damn you! How dare you repeat that to me. I know who those girls are. I wouldn't give a half-dime for any of them.'

'You got to see it soon, Molly. It's you and me that work together. It will always be that way.'

'Only in your dreams, Mr McComb. I see lots of young men I like the looks of. One just rode past here earlier this evening. Wearing rawhides. A new man?'

McComb looked away, and swore under his breath. 'We got a couple new ones.'

'What's his name? The young one?' She knew she was irritating him, and enjoyed it. McComb suddenly stood up and scowled down at her.

'You don't have to know the name of

every drifter that Walcott hires to do his shooting. Try to find some self respect, Molly, and some damn sense.'

Then he was storming off the porch, and out of the yard.

When he arrived back at the hunters' bunkhouse he got a surprise. Elias Walcott was there, and most of the riflemen, and Walcott had just begun addressing them. He turned when McComb walked in.

'Oh, good. I won't have to see you privately, McComb. I got some news. A rider come in with it earlier.'

McComb sat down on his bunk. O'Brien, Cahill and Navarro were all there, listening to Walcott.

'The rider was one of our scouts. He just rode in from an area south and west of here. About a day's ride, with our wagons. There's a herd there he says you can't see the other end of. They're grazing peacefully and will probably be there for several days.'

There was a low murmuring among the hunters. Walcott pulled a railroad watch from a pocket.

'It's almost nine. I want you all to be ready to ride out of here by midnight.'

'What?' McComb exclaimed.

'I know,' Walcott said. 'But an opportunity like this is rare nowadays. And there was no other hide company on it. I want us to be there about dawn tomorrow, or maybe a little later. I think we can do it if we ride hard all night.'

'Will we have grub out there?' a nearby hunter asked.

'I'll take the wagon,' Walcott replied. 'But there won't be no eating till the hunt's over. Any other questions?'

He looked around the room to a heavy silence. 'There will be plenty of ammo boxes loaded on the first hide wagon. I want you boys ready for a big spring kill.'

'I'll get them ready, Elias,' McComb said loudly. 'You can count on it.'

Walcott nodded and bowed his head. 'And God said, Let the earth bring forth living creatures for the use of man, and everything that creepeth upon the ground, and God saw that it was good. Amen.'

'Amen,' McComb repeated loudly. He turned and winked at Navarro.

'I'll see you all at midnight,' Walcott announced. 'And remember, this is why you pull down bigger pay than hiders. More is expected of you.'

When he was gone there was some mild grumbling about the midnight trek, but at twelve all were ready to ride, gathered in the compound on horseback.

O'Brien's appaloosa complained quietly to him for a few minutes, but then settled down.

By 12.30 by Walcott's watch the silent group of riders was through Ogallala and on the way south and west in a bright moonlight.

The trek was long and tedious. O'Brien and Cahill rode side by side, and Cahill related some stories about trapping in the Rockies to make the time pass more easily. O'Brien didn't understand the necessity, but didn't try to stop him. He was accustomed to riding all night for Wells Fargo, and before that while cattle droving. Once he had gone for three days and nights without sleep, food or water while stalking a killer grizzly for the Lakota.

Halfway through the night a few of the men began falling asleep in the saddle. One of them was so far gone that his mount started wandering off into the low hills away from the caravan of the riders and wagons. McComb saw it, and told Navarro, riding just behind him.

'I'll go round him up,' Navarro told him.

'No. Let the dumb jackass go. It will teach him a lesson.'

But a couple of minutes later O'Brien rode out to the sleeping hunter and came up beside his mount. He reached out and grabbed the sleeper, jerking him upright.

'Wake up, buffalo man. Or you'll miss the big show.'

McComb and Navarro both saw

what happened, and McComb just stared hostilely toward the two riders as they rejoined the others.

★ ★ ★

It was just at dawn when the company of riders crested a low hill and the herd came into sight. It was something few of them had ever seen before. In a long low valley the black, hulking shaggies carpeted the terrain like a thick blanket: it extended as far as the eye could see.

The long line of hunters drew up in a tight bunch, the wagons rumbling to a stop behind them. There was a long moment of absolute silence as everyone stared in awe. Then Walcott was at their fore, leaning on his saddle, a wide grin on his face.

'God has shown his mercy on us today, my lads.' He threw a small turkey feather into the air and it drifted away behind him. 'Good. The wind will not take our scent to them. Prepare for the attack.'

The sun was now climbing up from off the horizon behind them, making crimson stripes across the eastern sky. The buffalo came more clearly in view, and they were an impressive herd.

The hunters had formed a long line of attack now, and their mounts were guffering tensely. There was last minute loading of cartridges into chambers, and inserting of cartridges into belts.

'I ain't never seen a herd this big.' From one of the newer men.

'Look at them beautiful hides.' From the man next to him.

Down at the far end of the attack line, Cahill looked over at O'Brien.

'What do you think, partner?' he asked with a smile.

O'Brien was staring silently at the valley before him with its magnificent herd.

'This is what it was like,' he said quietly, 'before any of us got here.'

Fifty yards away, Walcott was ready to give the attack signal. He raised his arm high.

'And the fear of man and the dread of him shall be upon every beast of the earth. Genesis chapter nine, verse two. Now go show yourselves to the beast, and make him understand his fear.' Then his arm came down.

As on that day when Sam Spencer died, not long ago, the long line of riflemen thundered down a grassy slope toward the big herd. O'Brien and Cahill galloped along in their midst, and the appaloosa arrived at the herd out front. Now the air crackled and roared with hot gunfire as the riders merged with the frightened animals and began taking them down. O'Brien and Cahill were separated, and O'Brien was firing the Winchester over and over, barely taking aim to fire, hands free of the reins. Buffalo were going down all around him.

The noise was deafening. Dust rose into the air, restricting visibility. The herd stampeded in several directions as the shooting continued. A hunter on the edge of it all was knocked off his mount but was then rescued by another rider before he could be injured. Then the herd was disappearing into a rocky area beyond the hunters' reach.

Silence settled over them. O'Brien raised the Winchester's muzzle to the sky, and reined in. His kills lay all around the valley floor, almost two dozen in all, and almost twice as many as most of the others. Between 200 and 300 buffalo lay dead in high grass, except for a few that had to be dispatched with a shot to the head. Cahill rode over to O'Brien.

'Nice shooting, partner. I saw you working them.'

'I learned with the Lakota,' O'Brien said. 'They have to do it with arrows.'

Now Walcott rode past, just as McComb appeared near by.

'Great shooting, young man. You really earned your pay this day.'

McComb heard it, and grunted in his throat. O'Brien dismounted beside his latest kill.

'It's like shooting fish in a barrel,

ain't it?' He spoke without looking at Walcott.

Now everybody was on their feet, moving among the big, black humps on the ground, looking the hides over. Each man was supposed to skin and load the hides of the animals he himself had shot, but it rarely worked out like that. O'Brien stood over his biggest kill. He went and got a stake from his saddlebag and took a mallet from an equipment man who came past. Cahill walked over and helped O'Brien get the animal on to his belly, then O'Brien did the same for Cahill's first animal. O'Brien then returned to his animal and pegged the buffalo's snout to the ground with the iron stake. His next job was to make cuts behind the head and around where the legs joined the body. But suddenly McComb was standing beside him.

'Hold on there, O'Brien,' McComb said pleasantly. 'The boss wants me to give some instruction in stripping to newcomers. I'll do the first one for you.'

O'Brien gave him a quizzical look. 'The Lakota have a way of doing it pretty much like I see here,' he responded. 'I can handle it.'

'No, no,' McComb persisted, straddling O'Brien's buffalo. 'I don't want Walcott to think I'm shirking my duty.' He gave a hard grin.

In the next moment he was using a big Bowie skinning knife on the buffalo at the appropriate places. O'Brien was partly behind him, unable to see exactly how McComb was doing it, and that was the way McComb wanted it. He was just going through the motions of making deep cuts that would eventually separate the skin from the body of the buffalo. In a short time he stepped away from the animal.

'There. I got it done for you. Did you watch what I was doing there?'

O'Brien grunted. 'Much as I could.'

'Well, if you have any trouble with it, just come to me. Now I'll go skin a couple of my own kills.'

He walked away. O'Brien shook his

head. He brought the appaloosa over, tied a rope to a ring on the nose stake and the other to his saddlehorn and mounted the horse. Men all over the valley were doing the same. Now all he had to do was guide the horse past the animal's tail and then keep it walking away from it until the skin neatly ripped off the buffalo from neck to tail.

But as the appaloosa pulled on the rope, the hide did not separate. Now the whole bulk of the corpse was straining against the pull, and in the next moment the thick stake pulled loose from the ground, as the buffalo was rising off the grass. The horse had been pulling against the full weight of the animal, and had stalled in its tracks. Now it bucked for a moment as the corpse fell back to the ground on its side. The rope now hanging loose with the stake at its end, the horse was unfettered and O'Brien had to rein it in.

O'Brien turned the appaloosa and went back to the buffalo, the rope trailing behind him. The buffalo was all twisted around on the ground. He frowned heavily, dismounted and knelt to examine the buffalo. There were ragged edges where McComb was supposed to have cut neatly through the skin.

'Sonofabitch,' O'Brien muttered.

A couple of other hunters, situated near by, had turned to laugh at the mess O'Brien's animal was in. In the next moment Walcott rode up to O'Brien.

'What's the matter, O'Brien? Never skinned a shaggy before?' He smiled genially. O'Brien looked up at him somberly.

'I get it,' he said abruptly.

'We all have to learn the hard way,' Walcott told him. 'Just don't mind if the boys rib you about it. They don't know no better. You need any help now? I can get McComb over here.'

'I think I've got it now,' O'Brien replied.

Walcott nodded and rode on. A

moment later Uriah Cahill walked over as O'Brien was taking the stake rope over to the inert animal again.

'I saw the whole damn thing,' Cahill said when he arrived. 'That ornery bastard did that on purpose. To make it look bad.'

O'Brien looked across the high grass to where McComb was working on a buffalo, and saw the man grinning at him. Navarro, near by, was having a good laugh, and telling the man next to him about it. Cahill looked, too.

'See that? What did I tell you?'

'I see it,' O'Brien said.

'Well, did you tell Walcott?'

'It ain't Walcott's business. This is between McComb and me. It always has been from the minute we set eyes on each other.'

'Well,' Cahill said doubtfully.

'Here. Help me get this animal ready to skin,' O'Brien said.

4

There were a few more comments about the incident, at the hunt site and later in the barracks at Whiskey Creek. Other hunters would make joking comments, but all in good humour. Neither McComb nor O'Brien ever spoke of it. But McComb would often give O'Brien a crooked grin when he passed him.

The hunt they had just come off reaped big rewards for Walcott. Many of the hides were so-called robe quality, the very best hides that Plains Indians used for robes, boots and blankets. On the eastern market they would make Walcott a lot of money.

For days after the hunt hide-men were very busy scraping, tanning and currying the hides brought in on one of the big wagons. Most of the hunters, including O'Brien, were put to work stacking, sorting and recording hides already in the process that would make them ready for market. McComb was not required to participate in this work, but he came through the building regularly because he was technically their supervisor.

Two days after their return from the big hunt O'Brien and Cahill were working on stacking and counting hides in the warehouse building, when McComb came through. His friend the Mexican was working at a table of stacked hides not far from O'Brien and Cahill.

The stack of hides that O'Brien was counting was very high, and a bit unstable. McComb walked over to it, and spoke to O'Brien.

'What have they got you doing this for, greenhorn? You can't count to twenty without taking your boots off, can you?'

Near by, Navarro and another hunter laughed at the remark. Cahill, at the next table, scowled toward McComb.

O'Brien gave him an acid look.

'I'll manage all right.'

'You got this stack too high,' McComb went on. 'You don't want them on the floor. Walcott will begin wondering whether you're right for the job, after what happened on the hunt.'

'Ain't you got something to do?' O'Brien said, not looking at him.

'Maybe I'll just take a few of these hides off the top of the stack,' McComb said. Making sure O'Brien was standing close to the stack on the other side, he reached up and shoved the whole top part of the stack over toward O'Brien.

But O'Brien was looking at the stack at that moment, and saw them coming. He quickly stepped to one side as the heavy pile of hides brushed past him and hit the floor heavily beside him. He hurled a burning look at McComb.

'You bastard,' he growled.

'I was just trying to help,' McComb said, straight-faced. 'I told you they was stacked too high. It ain't my fault.'

O'Brien moved around the table and

came up very close to McComb. 'You keep at this, we're going to get into it, McComb.'

McComb unconsciously took a quick breath in. A moment later he hated himself for reacting. He got himself under control.

'Ain't you stretching the blanket some, rawhide? You're just a raw recruit talking to a foreman, remember? I can have your butt scraping hides if you ain't careful.'

'No, you can't,' O'Brien said in a low voice. 'I'd clerk in a general store before I'd scrape hides here.'

McComb grunted, 'Well, for now, get them hides picked up before Walcott sees them on the floor.'

'You pick them up,' O'Brien said evenly. 'You put them there.'

McCombs face colored. 'By God, I won't tell you again. Get them damn hides cleaned up!'

Cahill quickly stepped over to the table, near O'Brien, and lifted a hide up.

'I'm getting them, boss. I'm the one piled them that high, anyway. I'll load them onto my table. This boy can get on to more important work.'

McComb just stood there absorbing that for a moment. Cahill was a favourite with Walcott, and would listen to his view of things. Also, this allowed McComb a saving face without a showdown.

'Hey, if you want to do his work, go at it.' He gave O'Brien a last hard look. 'You're as good as gone, mister.' Then he turned and left the building.

That evening, after mess O'Brien and Cahill were in the bunkhouse sitting across a narrow aisle from each other. O'Brien had just finished oiling his rifle.

'If you want to do this for a while,' Cahill said to him, 'you're going to have to keep away for McComb. He likes to push his weight around. And you're his favourite target right now. He'll weary of it pretty soon.'

'It might not be soon enough,'

O'Brien said. He laid the Winchester aside, and stood up. 'I'm heading into town, Cahill. I'm getting a special scabbard made for my knife.'

'If you want to wait till I get a patch sewed on my shirt, I'll ride along.'

'No, I'll go it alone tonight. I'll see you back here in an hour or so.'

'I thought you had a knife sheath,' Cahill said.

'I'm having this one sewed onto my right stovepipe,' O'Brien said, referring to his boot. 'It might be handier for skinning.'

Cahill nodded. 'Never thought of that. Well, see you soon, partner.'

O'Brien saddled the appaloosa and rode into town a short time later. He was hoping a cobbler's shop was still open, even though it was dusk already. As he passed Elias Walcott's house, though, he heard Walcott calling his name.

'O'Brien. You have a minute?'

O'Brien reluctantly reined in. 'Sure, boss.'

He wrapped his reins over the hitching post out front and went up onto the wide porch, where Walcott stood smoking a pipe.

'Heading down to the Conestoga?' Walcott smiled at him.

'No, sir. Just getting some leather work done.'

Walcott lowered his voice. 'I know what happened the other day. With the skinning.'

O'Brien just stood there.

'Don't pay no mind to McComb. He gets out of line once in a while. But he's a good foreman.'

'A good foreman works with his men,' O'Brien said.

Walcott studied his strong face. 'I like you, boy. Try to find a way to fit in.'

Before O'Brien could reply a screen door opened and Molly Walcott came out onto the porch. Her face changed when she saw O'Brien. She looked him over carefully.

'Well. You're the one I saw ride past the other day. What's your name?' She spoke in a sexy, flirting manner.

'This here is O'Brien, Molly,' Walcott told her, smiling. 'Our new rifleman. He got us a pile of hides on that last hunt.'

Blonde Molly looked good in a tight gingham dress and with a bow in her hair.

'So you're a pretty good shot?' she purred at him.

O'Brien was getting uncomfortable. The only girls he had seen act this way were in saloons.

'Pretty good,' he finally said.

'That's a gross understatement.' Walcott grinned. 'I reckon he might be our very best rifleman.'

'Well I declare!' Molly said with a coy look. 'I thought you looked special when I first spotted you on that gray horse.'

Walcott looked over at his daughter and cleared his throat.

'Well, I'm going in to refill my pipe. Why don't you two go ahead and have palaver some?'

He left too abruptly for O'Brien to object and suddenly he was on the porch alone with Molly.

'Can you stay a minute or two?' she suggested.

O'Brien studied her pretty, sculpted face. He didn't recall meeting any female quite as attractive. And she was practiced at getting a man interested.

'I have to get to the cobbler before he closes,' he told her.

'Oh, he's open all evening,' Molly said. 'Why don't you set with me a minute. I'm not dangerous.' Another sexy smile.

O'Brien hesitated, and then he sighed inside. 'All right.'

They sat on the porch swing, and Molly sat down close to him. He could feel the soft touch of her beside him, and he liked it.

Molly asked him what he did before coming to Ogallala, and he told her briefly about Wells Fargo.

'Did you ever have to shoot anyone? I

mean, riding shotgun?'

'No, ma'am,' he said. 'It's mostly just boring trail stuff.'

'How tall are you?'

He looked over at her quizzically. 'I don't know, ma'am.'

'You must be one of the tallest men at Whiskey Creek,' she said.

He looked over at her. 'You grow up around here?'

'No, we had a ranch. Daddy came here a few years ago, when I was just growing breasts.' She put a hand over her mouth. 'Oh. I didn't mean to say that.'

'Yes, you did,' O'Brien told her.

She gave him a big smile. 'Yes, I did. That's because I like you, O'Brien. Better than all those other ones. You believe you can tell at first sight?'

'Tell what?'

'I had this feeling when you first rode by. It's kind of hard to explain. Would you like to kiss me?'

O'Brien smiled a rare smile. 'No, ma'am.'

'Why not? Don't you think I'm pretty?'

'You might be the prettiest girl I ever seen.'

'Well then.'

'You're the boss's daughter. And the boys say that you been seeing McComb. And I don't hardly know you, Molly.'

'Forget Cyrus! I just let him visit to keep from getting bored here. I would never think of him seriously.' She looked into his eyes. 'Like I would you.'

O'Brien rose. 'You don't know nothing about me, Molly. And now I got to get a scabbard made. I'm sure I'll see you around here again.'

She had risen, too. She stood very close to him and he could smell the aromatic perfume coming from her.

'You'd better,' she said in a pouting way. 'You're going to have to make up for tonight. Nobody has ever refused an invitation to kiss me, you know.'

'I believe that,' O'Brien said.

'Then you come visiting, you hear?'

O'Brien tipped his hat. 'I'll be by here, I'm certain. Good night, Molly.'

'I'll be thinking about you,' she said in that purring way.

Then O'Brien walked to the street and rode on into town.

* * *

Several days slipped past without any further word about shaggies in the area. O'Brien and Cahill worked steadily in the warehouse, without further trouble from McComb. Then one afternoon an older rifleman found McComb and told him he had seen O'Brien sitting on Walcott's porch with his daughter. McComb's face fell into hard lines.

'Are you sure?'

'I was just riding past on my way to the Conestoga. It was dark, but there was some light from inside the house. It was him, all right. I'd bet my next pay on it.'

'What the hell!' McComb hissed out. 'That brazen backwoods billy. That does it. I'll have that boy's ass.'

'I just thought you'd be interested,' the other man said.

Within a half-hour McComb found O'Brien taking cured hides off hangers in a back corner of the warehouse. He came over to him hostilely.

'What the hell do you mean, sneaking around sweet-talking Molly Walcott?'

O'Brien turned to him in surprise and wiped some sweat off his brow.

'Are you talking to me?'

'Don't play dumb, O'Brien. You was seen. Hanging around Molly like a bull in heat.'

'Oh. If you mean that set-down we had on Walcott's porch, I wasn't sneaking around, if that's any of your business.'

'You ain't got no reason to be at Walcott's house. Just what is it you think you're playing at?'

O'Brien let a long breath out. 'It was Walcott invited me,' he said casually. 'Now I got work to do, McComb.'

McComb's face changed. 'I don't

give that credence.'

O'Brien was getting irritated. 'I don't give a damn what you believe. What I do on my own time is my business.'

McComb stepped closer to him. 'You stay away from Molly Walcott, backwoods. You understand me?'

'Like I said,' O'Brien responded. Then he turned away to resume his work.

McComb lowered his tone. 'You get right in my craw, boy. You're right, this is going to come to a head.'

O'Brien took a hide down and laid it on a nearby table without even looking at McComb again. A moment later McComb was gone.

It was in late evening the next day, in the bunkhouse, when Uriah Cahill came over and sat beside O'Brien as O'Brien slid a big skinning knife in and out of its new scabbard on his stovepipe boot.

'That will work,' he said to himself.

'I heard about you and McComb,' Cahill told him. 'Navarro was talking to a confidant.'

'It ain't nothing,' O'Brien said. 'McComb is cow pucky with a loud mouth.'

'McComb is cow pucky with a gun,' Cahill corrected him. 'Listen, partner. I heard a couple of things. Walcott doesn't know it but McComb is wanted in three states in the south for murder and rape. He ain't somebody to get crossways of. He might just find an excuse to shoot you dead some dark night.'

'I don't think it will get to that,' O'Brien said.

'Just the same, I wish you'd go armed,' Cahill fretted.

O'Brien looked over at him. 'I never carried iron and I won't start because of some lowlife like McComb.'

'Then take your Winchester when you're in the Conestoga and other places. That would be something.'

O'Brien smiled at his concern. 'Look, partner. I know you like it here. But I might not be here much longer.'

Cahill frowned. 'Because of McComb?'

'Hell, no. I reckon I don't like company shooting, after seeing it up close. With up to five hundred buffs killed in one shoot it will all play out pretty fast with these methods. It's all too efficient. Companies even tanning their own hides now. Just a few years back, when I first come out here, I rode one day from Fort Hays to Fort Supply through buffalo all day. Already that's a thing of the past.'

'I know.'

'And that ain't all of it. The Lakota won't kill a calf. Or a young cow to preserve the herd for further hunting in the future. I see two calves down on that last hunt, and Walcott didn't seem to care.'

'Even the small hides will bring thirty dollars,' Cahill said. 'And that's what Walcott is geared to.'

'Well, I'll try to last it out a while. Me, I think I'd like to do some still shooting. On my own, or maybe with a partner. Crawl up close as possible on your belly and then start shooting from one position. Knocking off as many as you can before they realize what's happening. It needs real shooting know-how, of course. But you don't expose yourself or your mount to as much danger from stampeding.'

Cahill looked over at him. That was more talking than O'Brien had done in a week. He had obviously given the subject some thought.

'I think I could like that way.'

'It's real hunting,' O'Brien said. 'Next thing, the companies will be out there with Gatling guns.' He shook his head. 'I'd get me a Sharps .500. Hit a bull in the eye at a quarter-mile. I hear they got tripods now.'

'You been thinking on this quite a little.'

O'Brien shrugged. 'It buzzes in my head sometime.'

The next day at midday Walcott announced that another herd had been spotted, north and east of them. They would ride out the following day.

That evening O'Brien rode into town

alone, to get a spur repaired by the local blacksmith. On his way back to HQ, he saw Molly Walcott standing in her yard, picking an early rose for a vase inside the house. She looked up and saw him, and he reined in. The appaloosa guffered quietly.

'Hello, O'Brien. I knew you'd come by again.' She smiled widely. Her blonde hair was down on her shoulders and she looked especially pretty in the height of the setting sun.

O'Brien tipped his hat. He liked the looks of her, and her brashness.

'Molly. Just returning from town. Good to see you again.'

'Come on down off there and say hello properly,' she said with a smile. O'Brien hesitated, then dismounted. Inside the gate he walked over to her.

'I been thinking about you,' he told her. 'I have to admit it, you worry a man's blood, Molly.'

She gave him another big, wide smile. Then, suddenly, she reached up and planted a soft kiss on his mouth.

'Hey,' he said with a low chuckle. He was holding her close to him, and could feel the softness of her against him. 'What's that all about?'

'It means I like you, dummy,' she said. She didn't try to break away from him.

'I like you, too, Molly.' He released her reluctantly. 'But this is broad daylight out here.'

'It's the only chance I've had,' she said pertly. She looked him over. 'I liked it. I liked it a lot.'

'You move pretty fast, Molly.' He looked around to see if they were alone out there. 'You're always a little ahead of me.'

She put her arm in his. 'Would you escort me inside, kind sir?'

O'Brien found he liked having her arm in his. 'If you'll promise to behave in there.'

'Why, what an ungracious thing to say to a lady.'

'You talk funny sometimes, Molly.'

They walked into the house. Once

inside, Molly took him into the library
room where she had been with McComb
a few days ago. O'Brien stopped short
and stared at the opposite wall.

'Are them all really books?'

'Every one,' she replied.

'I only seen a half-dozen books in my
life,' he admitted.

'How many have you read?'

He hesitated, 'None.'

Molly looked into the deep-blue eyes.
'Well. There isn't much need for
book-reading in these parts. Let's set a
little.'

They sat together on a long sofa,
Molly placing herself so that she
touched him. He liked it, and let it
happen again.

'I don't have much time, Molly,' he
said. 'There's a big hunt tomorrow, and
I got things to do back there.'

'I won't keep you long. Say, you
never told me your first mane.'

'I don't use it.'

She frowned. 'It can't be that bad.
What is it?'

He looked over at her. 'I don't use it, Molly.'

'Goodness! All right, it's O'Brien. I'll get it out of you some day, though. I'm hoping there will be plenty of time.' A serious look met his gaze.

'Molly, what are you saying?'

'I've been thinking. I've never met anyone just like you. You do something to me, O'Brien. Something inside. Don't you feel it too?'

'I know I like you. I like you a lot.'

She looked away. 'You and me could own this whole thing some day. If it was right between us.'

O'Brien turned to her. She was a lovely girl, but when she talked this way, it took his breath away.

'Ain't you getting ahead of yourself just a little?' he suggested quietly.

'Not if you really like me. What I'm saying is, I think I'm falling in love. It's not like I wanted to. But these things just happen. I just hope you'll find the same feelings inside of you.'

O'Brien didn't know what to say. In

his young life he had never got close enough to any woman to take one seriously. He took a deep breath in.

'Molly. I'm still trying to find out what I want to do with my life. I'm kind of a loner. I'm most content when I'm out on the trail, hunkering down over a campfire and listening to coyotes yell at the moon. How would a woman fit into that world?'

'You would have that and me, working for Daddy,' she argued.

'I don't know how long that will be,' he told her. He stood up. 'I got to get back now. We can talk on this later if you still want to.'

She rose and faced him. Disappointment showed strongly in her pretty face.

'If you don't know now what you feel for me, maybe you never will.'

He didn't know how to respond to that. 'I never met a girl I liked more. You're different from the others. You say what you feel, and I like that. But I'm in no position to be long-thinking about much of anything just now. That could change, I know that. But that's all I can say right now.'

'Damn you, O'Brien!' Molly said loudly, and she was trying not to cry. 'Go hunt your damn buffalo.' She ran from the room.

★   ★   ★

It was raining when they started out the next morning, but about halfway to their destination the rain stopped and the sky began clearing. It took a while in the new area to find the herd, and it wasn't as big as the last one. Their clothing was drying out, and the mood among them was somber. As they lined up for the assault, McComb kept looking down the line of mounts toward O'Brien, but neither O'Brien nor Cahill were aware of it. Navarro was, but decided not to ask questions.

As usual, Walcott said a few words before they went, then they were thundering down on the herd, which was situated on rolling, uneven ground at the bottom of a butte.

The firing and yelling was raucous, and as the herd began stampeding all the other sound drowned out its roar. O'Brien and Cahill were separated, but both were finding regular targets. Buffalo were going down all around them, and a couple stumbled and fell over the rocky, bumpy terrain. In the middle of all that, McComb spurred his mount into a gallop directly at O'Brien's appaloosa.

O'Brien was in the act of putting his sights on a nearby bull, and did not see McComb coming. When McComb arrived at the appaloosa, he didn't rein in, but slammed his chestnut stallion into the side of O'Brien's mount.

The collision was violent and traumatic. The gray stallion jerked sideways, almost losing its footing. It threw O'Brien to one side. O'Brien caught the saddlehorn hard; he stopped his sidewise motion and managed to stay onboard. Only then did he see McComb beside him, and realized what had happened.

'Goddam you!' he yelled above the clamor around him.

McComb rode away, firing again at shaggies. O'Brien reined the big stallion in, made a couple more shots that took buffalo down, and moments later it was over. The herd was gone.

O'Brien sought out McComb then, and rode over to him. McComb was dismounting near a kill. He looked up at O'Brien.

'Sorry about that bump. My horse just got out of control for a minute there. Hell, you could of been trampled if you hadn't held on.' He gave a hard grin.

O'Brien had dismounted now, too. He strode over to McComb without speaking a word and threw a fist into McComb's face.

McComb felt as if he had been hit by a sledge hammer. He went flying over the hump of a dead shaggy and hit the ground hard on the other side. His nose was broken and blood ran down his face from it. He spat a tooth into the grass.

He was too stunned to say anything for a moment. Then his face slowly grew a deadly look. The look other men had just seen before their quick demise.

'Why, you mangy — ' he spat out breathlessly.

'Get up, you bastard, and I'll do it again,' O'Brien growled.

But now McComb drew the Colt Army .45 on his hip and aimed it at O'Brien's heart.

'Now you take a trip to hell, boy,' he grated out.

But Walcott had ridden over to them. He shouted at McComb.

'Hold it, McComb.'

McComb re-aimed. 'This is between me and him.'

Walcott quickly dismounted. 'You fire that thing, and you'll answer to me, by God!'

McComb's finger tightened on the trigger. But then he looked over at

113

Walcott. He was still on the ground.

'Do you see what he did to me?'

'Put the gun away,' Walcott said slowly.

McComb hesitated again, then holstered the big revolver. O'Brien had just stood silent through it all. Cahill walked over to them now, out of breath.

'McComb tried to knock O'Brien off his mount,' he yelled. McComb rose to his feet, staring fiercely at O'Brien.

'That's bull pucky,' he gritted out. 'My stallion lost its balance for a minute. I already told him.'

'You rammed me,' O'Brien now spoke up. 'You hoped I'd be trampled.'

Walcott looked over at McComb with narrowed eyes.

'Look, you two. I don't know what's going on here. But I want you to put an end to it.'

McComb's nose was swelling across his face. He felt where the tooth had come out of the corner of his mouth.

'You see this? And you want it to be done?'

'I'm going to skin my kills,' O'Brien said. He turned his back on all of them and walked away.

'This ain't over, rawhide,' McComb called after him.

'Get to work, McComb,' Walcott said heavily to him as he walked away.

5

When the hunting party arrived back at Whiskey Creek at the end of that long day O'Brien was at his bunk, cleaning the Winchester, when Cahill walked in and sat down on his bunk across from O'Brien. O'Brien did not acknowledge his presence. Cahill's middle-aged face looked particularly worn at that moment.

'McComb was going to kill you out there, wasn't he?'

'He was going to try,' O'Brien said, shoving a cleaning rod into the barrel of the long gun. Cahill grinned slightly. This was what he liked about O'Brien.

'Dawkins heard McComb talking to Navarro when they were skinning out there. McComb was saying how he's just waiting for his chance now. Talking about you.'

O'Brien laid the gun aside. 'He won't

be the first. Don't give it a second thought. I don't.

'He'll want to look good to Walcott. But he'll come for you, O'Brien. He's a born killer.'

'Well, he knows where to find me.' O'Brien went to a foot locker at the end of his bunk and got some things out of it. 'In the meantime, I'm giving Walcott my notice.'

Cahill's weathered face showed surprise. 'What?'

'I've had my fill of the hide company,' O'Brien said. 'I told you why. I'd like to try buffalo hunting. But on my own. Still shooting. I think I could make a living at it. Do better than my salary here maybe. And I wouldn't have to take no stupid orders from McComb. Or anybody.'

Cahill rubbed a hand across his mouth. 'Well.'

O'Brien looked up and saw Walcott coming down the aisle, congratulating hunters on their kills. He stopped at McComb's bunk for a moment and said a few quiet words to him, then came down the aisle. McComb looked down toward O'Brien's bunk. Then Walcott was standing before O'Brien and Cahill.

'You did some nice shooting again today,' he said to O'Brien. Then, turning to Cahill: 'You brought me a good one here, Uriah.'

Cahill nodded uncertainly. 'I thought you'd be pleased, Elias.'

O'Brien looked up at Walcott. 'I hope this don't disappoint you, boss. You been good to me. But I'm giving my notice. I'll stay till the end of the week and pick up my pay.'

Walcott slumped into himself. 'I hope this don't have nothing to do with McComb. I give him a talking to.'

'That boy will give you trouble as long as he's here,' O'Brien said. 'But he's only part of it. I want to go out on my own. I think I work better without somebody telling me what to do.'

'I could give you and Cahill a modest raise, if that will help keep you here.'

O'Brien shook his head. 'That ain't a factor. But thanks for the offer.'

Cahill was clasping and unclasping his thick hands. After a moment, he caught O'Brien's eye.

'If you could stomach a partner out there with you, 'I'd like to join you, O'Brien.'

'I'll be damned!' Walcott muttered.

O'Brien studied Cahill's face for a moment. 'I'd be pleasured to have you.'

Walcott grunted. 'I should have guessed that.' He puffed his cheeks out. 'I won't try to keep you here. But it won't be as pleasant a place without you.'

'We'll miss you, too, Elias,' Cahill told him.

Walcott met O'Brien's gaze. 'If you get a chance, you might tell Molly.' Then he added heavily, 'I think she's a little sweet on you, boy.'

'I'll stop past to say goodbye,' O'Brien said.

In the next three days O'Brien and

Cahill worked hard in the warehouse, piling and counting hides for the tannery, which was their last stop before shipment. McComb hadn't spoken to either of them since their return from the hunt, but on the last day he came over to O'Brien and spoke to him with a wide grin.

'I see you decided to run, boy.'

O'Brien looked up from sorting hides. 'Oh. You again. I don't know what the hell you're talking about.'

'I'm saying, I guess you took what I said seriously. Which you should.'

'I don't take nothing you say seriously,' O'Brien said. He took a robe-quality hide from a pile and put it on a smaller one. McComb leaned in toward him.

'You wouldn't a made it through the month here if you'd stayed.'

'Or you wouldn't,' O'Brien said coolly.

McComb shook his head slowly. 'Just run while you can, boy.' Giving a low chuckle, he turned and left.

* * *

That evening, their last at Whiskey Creek, O'Brien rode into town and visited Molly Walcott.

Her father was not there and O'Brien was ushered in by the maid. He found Molly in a spacious parlor, sitting in a chair near a fireplace in which a fire burned. She looked when he entered the room but did not rise or speak.

'Hello, Molly.' He held his Stetson in his hands. His long dark hair was slicked back, his mustache neatly combed.

She was angry, but she thought she had never seen so masculine a man.

'You wouldn't even have come by if Daddy hadn't suggested it, would you?'

'Of course I would,' he said quietly. 'Mind if I set down?'

'Suit yourself. You always do.'

He chose a chair facing her, and sat there, moving his hat in his hands.

'This wasn't an easy decision, Molly. I like Elias. And you.'

'If you liked me you'd stay here and make a life for us. I told you. There isn't anyone for me but you, O'Brien. I mean that.'

'This don't have to be the end for us,' he said. 'I'll be coming through here regular, I'm sure. I thought to see you then. We'd have more of a chance to get to know each other. I think that would be good.'

'I'll bet you'll come through here. Do you think I'm going to set here on my hands and hope you'll show up some day? I'm young, and I'm pretty. Men come courting regular here. Why, that Matt Dawkins was just here last night, sweet-talking me. Even though Cyrus warned him away. What do you think of that?' She demanded, sticking her chin out.

'I think it's about what you'd expect, Molly. You're the prettiest girl in town.'

'Do you know what I told Matt?'

'I wouldn't want to guess.'

'I told him I had a beau, and it was you. I said it was you.'

'Well. I'm sorry for Dawkins.' O'Brien offered, looking embarrassed.

'Oh, you are so frustrating!' she said loudly, looking away.

He sighed. 'Sorry I ain't quite what you expected,' he began. 'Look. I don't know what my future holds. But when I get through here again I hope I get to see you. That's what I stopped by to say.'

Molly rose and went to stand by the fire, her back to him. 'Without you here, things will be different. I might be in New Orleans by then. Singing at a dance hall for gamblers and sailors.'

O'Brien rose too, smiling 'I think that would surprise everybody.'

She turned to him. 'I mean it, O'Brien. This foolish decision of yours doesn't just change your life. It affects others, too.'

He was finished with it. 'Well, I'll be going. I'll look forward to seeing you soon, Molly. I've really enjoyed knowing you.'

'Oh, go to hell!' she blurted out, turning away again.

O'Brien turned too, then left the house.

When he arrived back at the compound Cahill was packing some gear into his bedroll in preparation for their morning departure. There were just a few other men there. O'Brien sat heavily on his bunk and Cahill glanced over at him.

'How'd your visit go?'

O'Brien gave him a sour look. 'Not so well.' He looked at the floor.

'Maybe I am being stupid, Cahill. I got a good-looking girl talking serious about me, and her daddy runs this whole damn place. Most men would think that's quite a step up.'

Cahill studied his somber face. 'Do you like her?'

O'Brien nodded. 'Yes. But I don't really know her.'

'You could end up owning this whole outfit.' Cahill grinned at him. 'Then you could give me a foreman's job.'

O'Brien returned the grin. 'You ain't no foreman.'

'You ain't no company owner.'

They exchanged small laughs.

'Well I'm ready to leave at dawn,' Cahill said. 'If you're still of a mind. But now, I'm going into town and get me a couple of swallows of red top rye while it's still available to us. Why don't you come along?'

'I don't know,' O'Brien said. 'I ain't got no interest.'

'Come on, partner. You need the fresh air. And I'm buying.'

O'Brien finally nodded. 'OK. That tipped the scales.'

When they passed by Walcott's house there was nobody on the porch. O'Brien was glad. A few minutes later they arrived at the Conestoga saloon. For the first time, because he knew it could be rowdy inside, O'Brien slid the Winchester from its saddle scabbard and took it inside with him.

Inside the saloon there were cowboys, town clerks and some of Walcott's men. O'Brien was pleased to see that McComb was not there. He and Cahill took a table near the front of the room, and ordered a bottle of rye whiskey. The piano player was taking a break, but the place was loud with the noise of conversation and laughter.

One of Walcott's hiders saw O'Brien from a back table, and held a glass of ale high.

'O'Brien! Hear you're heading out to hunt on your own. Good luck to you.'

'Yeah, good luck to both of you,' a companion called out.

Cahill nodded and lifted his glass. He was about to comment on the greeting when McComb and Navarro walked in just a short distance away. McComb saw O'Brien immediately.

'OK, hell!' O'Brien grumbled.

McComb got a hard grin on his thick features. The scar on his jaw and neck showed pink in the saloon lamps. He spotted a table behind theirs and he and Navarro took it. They sat down and spoke in low tones between themselves.

A waiter in an apron came over to them and wiped their table off with a cloth.

'What can I sell you tonight, gentlemen?'

McComb looked over at O'Brien's table. 'What are they having?'

'Why, I don't know, sir.'

'Hey, O'Brien! Cahill,' Navarro called out. 'What is your poison over there, muchachos?' A big grin accompanied these words.

McComb let his tongue move over the empty space at the corner of his mouth where O'Brien had knocked his tooth out. It didn't show unless he grinned widely. But it felt to him like a continuing insult and it festered deep in his gut. The swelling of his nose had gone down.

O'Brien didn't respond, but Cahill turned to them. 'We're having ourselfs a taste of rye over here, boys. Might be a little strong for you beer drinkers. I'd start off easy if I was you.'

'If you was me you could call yourself a man,' McComb barked out.

127

There was some laughter at the exchange from a nearby table.

'Just let it go, Cahill,' O'Brien said quietly. 'I'm trying to enjoy myself here.'

A hide man seated by the back wall yelled at McComb. 'Hey, McComb. Rawhide is leaving tomorrow. You ought to buy his drinks. You know, for old times' sake.'

There was another round of laughter at their table.

'You hear that, O'Brien?' McComb called over to him. 'The boys think I should buy your drinks. What do you think?'

O'Brien turned partly to him. 'I'd guess money holds to you like the cholera to an Apache,' he replied soberly.

McComb noticed the Winchester lying across the far side of O'Brien's table. He nudged Navarro and pointed at it.

'Look at that,' he said with a grin.
'What does he think he can do with

that in here?' Navarro replied quietly. 'I could put three holes in him before he found the trigger on that long gun.'

They were speaking so softly that O'Brien and Cahill couldn't hear them above the noise in the room. O'Brien was already sorry he had come. The liquor wasn't worth it.

'Hey, O'Brien,' Navarro called over again. 'I see you brought your buffalo gun in here. You expecting a herd to come through?'

There was more laughter, and now the saloon was warming to the exchanges.

O'Brien swigged a shot glass of whiskey like it was water, ignoring the Mexican. But Cahill was getting irritated, his weathered face looked sullen.

'Why don't you drink some little boy beer and keep it to yoursels?'

'Are you calling us little boys, old man?' McComb said in a hard voice. This would be a good chance to kill O'Brien, he realized. The hunter was armed, after all. He could tell Walcott any story he wished, after the fact.

'I call what I see,' Cahill replied.

O'Brien turned again to McComb. 'Let it go, McComb.'

Navarro took it up now, though. 'I don't think you should come in here and call names, *barrachos*. It could be . . . you know . . . dangerous.'

'It could be very dangerous,' McComb growled. He scraped his chair around so he was facing O'Brien directly. 'Maybe you shouldn't wait till tomorrow, backwoods, to leave. I think you ought to leave town tonight.' A hush had now fallen over the room. Glass tinkled when the bartender set a tankard down beside another one.

O'Brien had thought it would come to this. He put his hand on the rifle and moved its muzzle toward them slightly. McComb's dark eyes glistened with hatred as his hand went out over his gun. But Navarro was very excited about developments.

'No, wait, *amigo*. Remember Walcott and your position.'

'Better listen to the greaser, McComb,' O'Brien responded. 'It could be the best advice you had in a while.'

McComb saw the look in O'Brien's eyes, and hesitated. In that moment, Navarro rose from his chair.

'You call me a greaser, you trail scum!' His hand reached for the Remington Army .44 at his hip.

But before his hand reached the gun O'Brien fired the Winchester and it roared in the room. The lead cut Navarro's holster from its belt and it fell heavily to the floor with the gun still in it before Navarro could get at it.

O'Brien had not moved from a sitting position, the Winchester now lay on the table, his finger in the trigger assembly.

Navarro stared at his gun on the floor wide-eyed. '*Dios mio*!' he whispered.

McComb's eyes narrowed on O'Brien as he sat tense, on his chair.

Then there was a burst of laughter around the room, a release of the built-up tension.

McComb looked around the room, hot anger in him. His hand was still out over his deadly Colt. The laughter subsided. McComb looked ready to act.

'Go ahead,' O'Brien told him. He rose slowly and stood facing McComb, the rifle held loosely in his grasp. 'Let's see how it plays out.'

McComb stood up as silence filled the room again. His hand twitched, hanging over the Colt. Then he dropped it to his side. He reached out, picked up a beer glass and threw it violently to the floor. Where it smashed loudly.

He was breathing shallowly. 'Get your goddam gun and let's get out of here,' he said in a snarl to Navarro. Navarro gave O'Brien a wary look and got his gun. Then he was following McComb out through the swinging doors.

'Don't get lost out there in the dark,' Cahill called after them.

There was no reply.

6

Cahill half-expected an ambush by McComb and Navarro on their way back to Whiskey Creek that night, but they arrived safely at the compound. O'Brien didn't think McComb would try anything at company HQ, but he and Cahill took turns standing watch. McComb and the Mexican didn't show up until later, and made no move against them.

By sunrise O'Brien and Cahill were saddled up and ready to ride out. Walcott and several other men were outside to see them off. Walcott wished them well again, and after he had gone back inside McComb showed up. He walked over to O'Brien, who was now mounted.

'A word of advice, O'Brien. If you really intend to hunt shaggies out there, keep out of our way. I won't ever want to see you on one of our herds. If I do, you're a dead man.'

O'Brien met his gaze with a cool one. 'We'll hunt where the herds take us, McComb. And I hope Walcott fires you before you cause any more trouble here.'

'Don't count on it,' McComb told him.

Then they were gone.

For the next three days they rode south and into Kansas, purposely to put themselves outside the range of Walcott's operations. They travelled so as to avoid riding through towns, making hardship camp every night, eating beans out of a tin and roasting rabbit over a crackling fire with a green stick. Both men preferred that to town life. Later when they had bought more provisions, there would be corn dodgers, tinned fruit and chicory coffee.

They eventually stopped in a small town north of Wichita called Smith Junction, to buy supplies. They spent the next couple of days purchasing food supplies, a beat up old wagon for hides, a long-eared mule to haul it and camp equipment. At a gun store they bought ammunition and asked to see some larger-calibre rifles. The clerk brought out two Sharps .500 rifles and showed them.

'You want these for buff hunting?' the gray-haired fellow asked.

O'Brien nodded. 'That's right.'

'Well, this here is the biggest gun on the market. Powerful. Accurate up to a quarter-mile in the right hands. Not too heavy neither. Nice balance.'

'Just let me see the gun,' O'Brien said, taking one from him.

He hefted it and sighted it on a lamp post outside. He looked it over carefully. He nodded and gave it to Cahill.

'What do you think?'

Cahill took it and smiled. 'It's a lot of gun for an old man. But I like it.'

'We'll take both of them,' O'Brien said. 'And five hundred rounds of ammo for them.' They had already

135

purchased ammo for their other rifles.

'Five hundred? I don't know if I got that much.'

'Give us what you got,' Cahill said.

'And the scabbards,' O'Brien added. 'Can you get them attached to the saddles?'

The clerk nodded. 'I'll have them ready for you tomorrow early.'

O'Brien sighed. That meant a night in town. 'You got a deal.'

'We rode in from the north,' Cahill said. 'Didn't spot any herds. How's the hunting in these parts?'

The clerk arched his eyebrows. 'None better, boys. They been taking a lot of hides south and east of here. Big herds. But of course not like ten years ago.'

'Sounds good enough,' Cahill told him. 'We'll pick up this stuff tomorrow.'

There was a small hotel down the street, and the pair took a room on the first floor. But not until after a small dispute.

'We'll take a room. Two beds,' O'Brien told the desk clerk.

The reception area was high-class, with potted palms and a carpet on the floor. There was a Remington painting on the far wall. The clerk looked the two over carefully.

'You sure you came to the right place, gentlemen?' he said warily. 'There's an inexpensive rooming house just down the street.'

'We can afford this,' Cahill said acidly.

'Well, if you're sure. We send all of you trail people down the street. You get your breakfast free there.'

O'Brien gave him a perturbed look. 'You got good hearing, mister?'

The clerk gave a nervous smile. 'Oh. Yes. Well, I could give you a room upstairs. At the rear. I think that would suit your purpose.'

'Just give us the key,' Cahill said even more acidly.

When they got to the room Cahill threw himself onto one of the two beds.

'My God. I never been on this soft a mattress.'

O'Brien pushed a hand onto his, and shook his head. He grabbed a pillow and threw it onto the floor beside the bed.

'I can't sleep on that. I'll sleep on the floor.'

Cahill gave him a surprised look, then grinned.

'You must of been with them Lakota longer than I figured.'

They had brought their rifles from their horses' saddler. O'Brien retrieved his from a corner of the room and sat in a chair with it. He 'broke' the long gun with a release device and peered through its barrel. Cahill had picked up a Kansas City newspaper that some previous tenant had left behind. He was reading the headlines.

'Anything happening in the big world out there?' O'Brien asked, snapping the rifle back into lock position.

'Somebody named Mark Twain just published a book called *The Gilded Age*. Whatever that means.'

'Never heard of him,' O'Brien commented.

'Jesse James held up a bank in Russellville, Kentucky.' Cahill grinned. 'That boy is making a name for hisself.'

'Never met a gunfighter I liked,' O'Brien said. 'Did you clean that Hotchkiss?'

'I ain't fired it,' Cahill replied. 'Hey, here's one. The price of robe-quality hides has gone up to sixty dollars in Boston. They're even paying thirty for green hides at the Fort Griffin market. Walcott will get rich if this keeps up. Maybe we'll even get in on some of it.'

O'Brien stared across the room. Remembering how embarrassed he had been when Molly found out he couldn't read. He glanced over at Cahill reading the paper.

'Maybe one of these days. When we got the time.'

Cahill looked over at him. 'What?'

'You could show me. A little about how that's done.'

Cahill understood. 'Reading?'

'Just so I could read headlines and stuff.' He was looking down at his rifle.

Cahill's lined face softened almost unnoticeably. He had never heard O'Brien ask for help in anything. It touched him emotionally. He cleared his throat.

'Of course. It would pleasure me to help. It ain't nothing really.'

'Just a smattering is all I'd need. I ain't planning to read no books.'

'I'll pick up a *McGuffy's First Reader* before we ride out,' Cahill said. Then he shook his head.

'What?' O'Brien said warily.

'I was just thinking. You speak three Indian languages. You taught Gray Hawk how to make cartridges and field strip a rifle. You can hunt and track like a Cherokee. And you've won prizes at target shoots. And behold! I can teach you something.' He laughed softly.

O'Brien grunted. 'Don't push that line too far, partner, or you'll have to digest that newspaper.'

Then they both had a quiet laugh.

They ate at a small café across the street that evening, and Cahill was glad to get a break from the trail grub. O'Brien had a big steak, six eggs and fried potatoes. Then they returned to the gun store and O'Brien bought a tripod for the Sharps rifle.

'My eyes ain't good enough to shoot so far that would do me any good,' Cahill declared.

'In case you're interested,' the owner said, 'a cowpoke that come in earlier said a pretty nice little herd was spotted west of here less than a day's ride. Out past Smith Meadows.'

'Is everything hereabouts called Smith?' Cahill said.

'Just about.'

'Appreciate the report on shaggies,' O'Brien told him. 'Maybe we'll look into it.'

By dawn the following morning, they were on their way west.

It only took to mid-afternoon to find the herd. It was small, less than 200 animals. But it was enough for two men still-shooting. They were able to get close enough so O'Brien didn't use his tripod. But the big Sharps rifles boomed out again and again before the herd ran. O'Brien had taken down six, and Cahill four. They couldn't have done that with the Winchester and the Hotchkiss.

The rest of that day was spent skinning and scraping and loading the hides onto their wagon, while the mule stood patiently waiting near the picketed mounts. Not long afterward they found a small stream where they watered the animals and cleaned themselves up. It was too late to return to Smith Junction, where there was a small market for green hides, so they made camp at the stream.

It was dark when they got a fire going and fired up some beef jerky. O'Brien had a couple of corn dodgers with it, but Cahill declined.

'I went four weeks once in the mountains with nothing to eat but corn dodgers. At the end I got the corn bread heaves. I ain't ate much of it since.'

'We can get some wheat flour,' O'Brien suggested.

Cahill looked up at a bright moon overhead. 'You know, it don't get any better than this.'

O'Brien swigged some coffee and looked over at him. 'It beats clerking in a Kansas City bank.'

Cahill grinned, 'I mean it. This is what I was born for. I hope it goes on for ever.'

O'Brien looked into his cup. 'Nothing goes on for ever,' he said softly.

Cahill squinted down on him. It was unusual to hear something like that from a young man in his twenties. But O'Brien had already seen a lot of life in his young years. And death. Cahill was about to respond to that when they both heard the sound of hoofbeats coming toward camp.

Cahill always carried a sidearm. He rose and drew a Starr .44 from its holster. O'Brien just sat there waiting.

In a couple minutes a pudgy, sloppy-looking rider came into the firelight, riding a dun mare. He gave them a big grin.

'Evening, strangers.' He saw the gun. 'No need for that, boys. I'm just a poor Bible drummer on his way to save some sinners in Wichita.'

O'Brien shook his head, and Cahill holstered his weapon.

'You almost sold your last Bible, mister. You in need of a cup of coffee?'

The overweight drummer dismounted. His face was round and flabby and his fancy boots looked like they had been bought in Boston. He spoke in a high, squeaky-sounding voice that irritated the ears.

'I would like nothing better.' He came over and took a cup proffered by Cahill. Cahill sat back down on his saddle and the newcomer stood.

'God bless you, gentlemen,' he said in his squeaky voice. He swigged the coffee thirstily, then wiped his mouth with a sleeve. 'Say, maybe one of you would like a copy of the Good Book.' He looked down at O'Brien, 'Have you been saved by our Lord Jesus Christ, young man?'

O'Brien gave him a look that made the drummer wince.

'Well. Not everybody is ready for redemption,' the young man concluded.

Cahill smiled. 'Have a corn dodger. It will make your bowels move.'

The visitor gave a half-smile. 'Don't mind if I do.'

'Don't drop it. It could break a toe,' Cahill added sourly.

The drummer brought a Bible case from his mount and sat on it by the fire. He ate the corn muffin and drank the rest of the coffee. The other two men appreciated the silence. But it didn't last long.

'My name is Funk. Wesley Funk. From New Orleans by way of Abilene.' A wry smile played over his face. 'Who do I have the pleasure to sit with?'

O'Brien sighed. 'Ain't you about finished with that coffee?'

Funk caught his gaze. 'Oh. Of course.' He threw the remainder onto the ground, and set the cup down. 'I was just wondering. I saw the hide wagon over there, and thought you might be buffalo hunters.'

'What if we was?' Cahill said.

'Well, I talked to this drifter yesterday. He said he'd just seen a big herd way up north of here, by the Nebraska border. Just thought you might like to know.' He rose and picked up his case. 'This fellow was mighty impressed.'

O'Brien and Cahill exchanged looks as Funk arranged the case again on his mount's flank.

'Did this boy seem pretty sure about all that?' Cahill asked. Funk assured them that he had, a few minutes later he was gone. O'Brien poked a stick at the fire.

'That's way out of range.' Cahill shrugged. 'It's just a couple days ride with the wagon.'

O'Brien hesitated, then nodded. 'What else we got to do? But let's make tracks a couple hours before dawn, partner. It will give us a leg up.'

'I'll be ready to ride.' Cahill grinned.

★ ★ ★

Out at Whiskey Creek outside Ogallala, a scout had just ridden up outside Elias Walcott's office. He now found Walcott at a desk, making out shipment orders. Walcott looked up at him quizzically.

'Hollis. Didn't expect to see you back here so soon. See anything worth hunting out there?'

Hollis shook his head. 'Just a scattering of small bunches. But I talked to a fellow that had just come up from the south. He says he just saw a really big herd down by the Dawson Flats. I thought you ought to know.'

Walcott frowned and sat back on his chair. 'Why, that's halfway to Wichita! On the Kansas border.'

'I know. But if the herd is big enough it would pay to go that far.'

Walcott pursed his lips. 'That would

147

be two days' ride.'

At that moment Cyrus McComb walked in behind Hollis. He looked disgruntled. He had failed to receive a raise in pay he had expected, and which he had planned to brag about to Molly. But Walcott said that profits were down and he would have to wait. Also, McComb had had an altercation with the hunter Flannery, and Flannery had quit, meaning McComb had to recruit another man. He was in a foul mood.

'McComb,' Hollis greeted him.

McComb cast a quick glance at him. 'Yeah, Hollis. Listen,' turning to Walcott, 'them new scrapers don't know what the hell they're doing, Elias. They're passing stuff on that won't never get to the tannery.'

Walcott arched an eye-brow. 'Well. I'll have to speak to the foreman.'

'I talked to the foreman. I don't think he cares what goes through there.'

'Well, I'll straighten him out, McComb. Look. Hollis here has some news for us. There's supposed to be a big herd way south of here, down by Kansas.'

McComb was still frowning. 'Then let some other outfit handle it. That would be a big, expensive haul for us.'

'Maybe the herd would pay for it,' Walcott argued. 'We haven't had a good hunt lately.'

McComb stood there thinking. 'This place is driving me crazy lately. Maybe I need a good long outing.'

Walcott nodded. 'Then it's settled, Hollis. Get your people ready, McComb. We'll leave early tomorrow.'

McComb nodded. 'Let's do it,' he said curtly. Then he turned and left.

A few hours later, just at dusk, McComb knocked on Molly Walcott's front door. She answered it herself. When she saw who it was, her face fell.

'Oh. It's you.'

'I'd like to talk a few minutes, Molly.'

She stepped out onto the porch. 'We can do it out here,' she said. Her blonde hair was up in a twist behind her head,

149

and she looked particularly good to him.

He came close to her. 'I been coming here too much without any serious talk by you. You keep putting me off, girl. When are you going to start thinking of me like a respectable suitor? We're going off for a few days tomorrow, and I'd like to carry something away with me I can hold close.'

Molly sighed. 'I've tried to tell you, Cyrus. But you haven't been listening. There will never be anything between us. You're too old for me. I've been going to tell you this for some time now. I want you to stop coming by.'

He looked as if she had slapped him in the face. His already dark mood instantly became darker. He grabbed her shoulders fiercely.

'Have you been playing me along, damn you? With your flirting and cute talk! Have you settled on somebody else and kept it to yourself?'

She shrugged. 'I kind of thought I

might wait for O'Brien to show up again here.'

McComb's eyes took on a deadly look. 'O'Brien? O'Brien!'

'I like him,' she said. 'I might be in love.'

McComb could hardly contain himself. He threw her away from him.

'You goddam man-teaser! What have you been doing with that backwoods billy? You had everybody thinking you was a good girl. And look what you was doing behind our backs.'

'I saw him openly,' Molly said, a little frightened of him. 'And I have nothing to be ashamed of. Now, I think you'd better leave, Cyrus.'

He was breathing shallowly. He raised a fist as if to strike her, but then dropped it heavily to his side.

'I wouldn't touch you now with a ten-foot pole,' he hissed at her.

When he was gone she stood there with a hand on her breast, her heart pounding in her chest. She was glad she'd seen the last of Cyrus McComb.

* * *

Two days later, in a broad valley in the uppermost reaches of Kansas, O'Brien and Cahill dismounted from their horses and stared in satisfaction at the large herd of buffalo before them, about 200 yards distant. They were filling most of the large open meadow.

'Is that a beautiful sight?' Cahill grinned.

'The wind is right,' O'Brien said. 'I'm setting up.'

They picketed their mounts to ground stakes close to the mule and wagon, and moved forward to get themselves into position. O'Brien set up his tripod and affixed the Sharps to it. Cahill drew his own Sharps and knelt on one knee.

The herd were grazing peacefully into a soft breeze blowing from the opposite direction. A big bull with a robe-quality coat turned and looked directly at O'Brien, but did not understand what he was seeing. His nostrils glistened in the early-morning sun, and he snorted softly.

The herd wasn't as big as reported, but it would offer good shooting. O'Brien knelt behind his Sharps and sighted in on a bull far on the other side of the herd. He would leave the close-side ones to Cahill.

Then the big guns began booming out into the quiet of the valley. Again and again they roared out their message to the morning, and one by one the buffs began falling in the herd. A few began running, but most stayed. The hunters fired again and again, and finally the herd stampeded away over a low hill.

Twenty buffalo lay dead in the high, dew-soaked grass. O'Brien could still smell the acrid odor of gunsmoke in the air.

'Our best haul yet,' Cahill called over to O'Brien. 'We're going to get rich, by God!'

O'Brien smiled his rare smile. 'A good hunt,' he agreed.

But at that same moment, the entire company of Walcott's hunters was emerging from behind an outcropping of rocks, just coming in sight of the corpse-littered valley floor.

Over at the kills O'Brien and Cahill were just taking a close look at a big bull with a fine coat of robe quality. O'Brien was kneeling down by the animal, and Cahill was still standing.

'It's a damn beauty,' O'Brien was saying to his partner.

Up on the higher ground near by, the wagons of Walcott's party were rolling up behind the forerunners. O'Brien, down at the buffs, put his hand to the ground and felt it tremble.

The first of Walcott's hunters on the scene were McComb and a couple of other men. When McComb saw the littered valley with the herd gone, and O'Brien and Cahill in among the shot animals, his face twisted into a mask of pure rage. He swore loudly.

'I don't by God believe it!'

O'Brien looked up now. He squinted

toward the newcomers. Cahill followed his gaze.

'Oh-oh,' he muttered. 'It's Walcott's party.'

Up on the high ground McComb was fuming.

'I told that bastard what I'd do if he ever ruined a hunt for us.'

Navarro had ridden up beside him. '*Que Diablo!*' he muttered.

In a swift movement, McComb slid his rifle from its saddle scabbard and levelled it on the two hunters. O'Brien was almost hidden behind the bulk of the dead buffalo, so he zeroed in on Cahill first.

'What the hell!' O'Brien exclaimed, rising to his feet. 'Cahill! Get down!'

But it was too late. McComb's rifle roared out loudly, and Cahill felt the hot lead hit him like a club in the chest. The cartridge missed his heart by an inch, busting his ribs and collapsing his lung as it passed completely through him. He was jerked violently off his feet, and thrown hard to the ground near O'Brien. O'Brien was stunned.

'Cahill!' he yelled out. Then he saw McComb's rifle aimed directly at himself.

Just as McComb's gun roared again O'Brien dived to the ground. He felt the lead graze his left shoulder as he went down.

Up on the rise of ground McComb was swearing again, and setting his sights once more. He found the prone O'Brien and put his sights on his head.

Then Walcott rode up. He knocked the muzzle of McComb's rifle aside, causing the shot to go wild.

'Goddam it!' McComb yelled.

But Walcott was angry, too. 'What the hell is the matter with you, McComb?'

O'Brien was going for his mount now.

'They stole our herd!' McComb yelled again. 'Let me take him down while we can.'

'We don't kill because somebody beats us to a herd!' Walcott barked into his face. The other hunters sat their mounts in stony silence, watching. 'Put that damn rifle away or I'll shoot you myself! You're fired, mister.'

McComb kept the rifle raised, watching O'Brien from the corner of his eye. 'You think I'd go on working for a man that won't defend his territory? To hell with you, and to hell with the company!'

Walcott looked toward O'Brien, who had retrieved his rifle and had turned to confront McComb.

'Hold it, O'Brien! He's disarming himself.'

O'Brien didn't care. He aimed the Winchester at McComb. But McComb slid his rifle back into its scabbard.

'You going to shoot an unarmed man, Rawhide?' he called, a glittery grin on his face.

O'Brien hesitated, then dropped the muzzle of the long gun.

McComb turned to Navarro. 'You coming?'

Navarro nodded.

'See you in hell, Walcott,' McComb said loudly.

'Should we stop him, boss?' young Dawkins asked tensely. He was sitting his mount near Walcott. Walcott shook his head.

McComb and Navarro were galloping off over a rise of ground. O'Brien was almost ready to board the appaloosa to ride after them, but then looked over at his partner, who was still alive.

O'Brien heaved out a breath, walked over and bent down to look at Cahill. There was a lot of blood. Cahill was making rasping noises in his throat. He tried a grin for O'Brien that didn't work.

'I knew — that bastard — would be trouble.'

'Lay still. We'll get you to a doc.' A lump came in his throat.

'Well — we had a good run, didn't we?'

'It's been an honor riding with you, partner. Here comes Walcott. He'll get you some help.'

Cahill tried to shake his head. 'I don't need — help — I need — rest.' Then a great rattling came from his lungs, and he was dead. O'Brien looked up. Walcott was standing over him.

'I'm real sorry, O'Brien. I reckon it's my fault. I knew McComb was no good.'

'No, it's McComb,' O'Brien said solemnly. 'It was always McComb. And it was always me had to deal with it. I don't care if that bastard rides to Alaska. Or China. He'll pay for what he done here.'

7

Walcott persuaded O'Brien to let him bury Cahill in Ogallala and O'Brien decided to accompany the party back there for the funeral. It took place on a dull day out at Boot Hill. Walcott himself presided.

'Blessed be the God and Father of our Lord Jesus Christ, for according to his great mercy he gave us a new birth to a living hope through the resurrection of Jesus Christ from the dead. Ashes to ashes. Dust to dust.'

He and O'Brien threw a handful of dirt down onto the coffin, a gesture that was followed by a number of company men.

O'Brien was offered his old bunk for the night, as he intended leaving early the next morning. After the evening meal Walcott asked O'Brien into his private office. When he was seated across from Walcott at his desk, Walcott regarded O'Brien seriously.

'You're going after him, ain't you?'

'That's my plan.'

'Vengeance is mine, sayeth the Lord.'

'This ain't vengeance. I can't do nothing for Cahill now. This thing grew up between McComb and me way before this. But this brought it all to a head. Now, it's him or me.'

'You know, young fellow, you could be the best I ever had. You could make a future here. A big future. Why don't you let this go? McComb will get his just deserts one day soon. It don't have to be you.'

'Yes it does,' O'Brien said.

'Will you think on coming back here? When it's over?'

'That's too much to put my head on,' O'Brien told him.

'Well I hope to see you back here some day. That's an invitation.'

'It's appreciated,' O'Brien told him. 'Now, I'm going to tend to my equipment.' They had both risen from their chairs when quite unexpectedly Molly came through the door.

'Well, good evening, daughter,' Walcott smiled a tired smile. 'I wonder what brings you out here?' He grinned at O'Brien.

'I heard you were here,' she said to O'Brien. 'You said you'd stop by if you got back here.'

'I was planning to see you,' he said.

'Well, maybe I'll just leave you two and take a look at some hides,' Walcott said. 'See you before you leave, O'Brien.'

O'Brien nodded, and Walcott was gone. Molly sat down on her father's chair and O'Brien resumed his own seat.

'You're looking good, Molly.' He smiled at her.

She looked down. 'Daddy offered you your job back, didn't he?'

O'Brien nodded. 'Yes he did.'

'And you said no.'

O'Brien regarded her soberly. 'Molly, things have changed. My life has changed.'

'Daddy said you might go after McComb.'

He looked down at his hands.

'I'm sorry about your partner,' she told him.

O'Brien looked up. She seemed different, too. Maybe more mature.

'Stuff happens in life. I lost my folks back in the Shenandoah. When I was just a kid. You just go on.'

'Is it still like you said? With you and me?' she asked quietly.

He sighed. 'You know how much I like you, Molly. That ain't never going to change. But I'm going to level with you, you deserve it. Whatever happens with me and McComb, I might never get back to Ogallala now.'

She felt dampness in her eyes. 'That's what I thought,' she said.

'Some things just don't work out like you might want,' he added.

There was a long silence between them. At last, Molly spoke.

'Young Matt Dawkins has been coming around regular,' she said, almost inaudibly. 'I haven't known how to handle that — because of you.'

O'Brien held her gaze silently.

'Just before you all arrived back here, Matt asked me to marry him.'

O'Brien looked past her, across the room. It was unexpected, but he felt a moment of envy inside him. Molly was peeking at him for his reaction.

He looked back at her, at the pretty face, the blonde hair, the look of hope still in her blue eyes. Wishing he had met her later, when he had found out who he was.

'Dawkins would be good for you, Molly,' he heard himself say.

When Molly looked up again a tear ran down her cheek. 'He comes from a good family, and he's very likeable.' She gave a heavy sigh. 'I guess I'll have to think seriously on it.'

'I hope you do.'

Molly brushed at a damp place on her cheek, and rose. O'Brien stood, too.

'I have to get back, O'Brien.' She looked deep into his blue eyes. 'If you never get back here, I wish you well.'

'And I hope you make a fine life for yourself,' he told her, the words coming out bitter to him. 'That would please me.'

She started to respond, but couldn't. She started to cry, so she turned and hurried from the office.

O'Brien figured he would never see her again.

★   ★   ★

That evening in the bunkhouse, O'Brien couldn't look at Cahill's old bunk. He was just pulling his stovepipe boots off when Walcott stopped past. He had a frown on his face.

'Molly told me that just an hour ago she accepted a proposal of marriage from Matt Dawkins. Frankly, that surprised me, O'Brien.

'I think Molly and me both know my future don't hold no place for women,' O'Brien said heavily. 'I regret that,

165

Walcott. You got a fine girl there.'

Walcott nodded somberly. 'Well. What is, is. I wish it could have been another way. But God has his plans for us.'

'I'll miss both of you,' O'Brien said.

'Anyway, I got some news for you. I got this from Dawkins, as a matter of fact. Before Flannery left, he overheard McComb say to Navarro that he wanted to get back to Billings, Montana, some day. Said he had some wild days there when he was younger. He might just be heading in that direction now. Just a guess, but I thought you ought to know.'

O'Brien nodded. 'Sounds like a good lead. Listen, if I don't see you tomorrow morning, Walcott, it's been a pleasure knowing you.'

Walcott took his hand, and felt the iron grip.

'The same goes for me, O'Brien. Be careful.'

O'Brien smiled. 'I expect to.'

O'Brien was gone the next morning two hours before dawn, and without saying another word to anybody there.

He decided to proceed on the assumption that McComb and Navarro were headed to Billings in Montana, unless for some reason he came across any evidence that pointed him in another direction. At a small frontier town in eastern Wyoming, O'Brien inquired at a local saloon. Two men of McComb's and Navarro's description had been in there several days ago, raising hell and shooting the place up. He knew he was on the right track.

After he had obtained that information from the bartender O'Brien ordered a bottle of planters' rye and took a seat at a table. But he had barely sat down when a tall man in a dark suit seated at a nearby table called out to the bartender.

'Don't serve that fellow that whiskey, barkeep.'

O'Brien looked over there and saw who was speaking. The tall man was sitting with two others; they looked like ranch hands. The tall man was apparently the rancher.

'That's right, I'm talking about you,' he said in a low growl.

O'Brien narrowed his eyes, looking the three of them over. This was why he preferred hardship camp to towns. You had to deal with all kinds of humanity in places like this. He didn't have the patience for it. He turned back to the bartender.

'I think you heard me, bartender. A bottle of planters', and a glass.'

The bartender glanced at the rifle O'Brien had laid on the table beside him, and looked fearfully over to the rancher.

'You heard me, too,' the tall man said. 'You serve that man, and I'll have to have my boys commence on you.'

O'Brien turned a stony look on him. 'What the hell are you up to, mister?'

The rancher downed a shot glass of

whiskey. 'You're a buffalo hunter, aren't you?'

O'Brien thought about that a minute. 'I guess I am.'

'A few weeks ago a few of my cattle strayed into buffalo country, and some men just like you shot and slaughtered them cattle with my brand on them.'

'What's that got to do with me?' O'Brien said.

'You're a buffalo hunter. They're all alike in my book.'

'Yeah. All alike,' one of his men echoed arrogantly.

O'Brien grunted. 'You boys are feeling a mite juicy, ain't you?'

'We just don't drink in the same establishment with buffalo hunters,' the rancher responded. 'Now, since you can't drink here, I suggest you haul your carcass out of here while we're still in a fairly good mood.'

O'Brien sighed heavily. He rose from the table, and picked up the Winchester.

'Good.' The rancher smiled. 'You got

more sense than I figured. Go chew on some buffalo hide.'

He laughed in his throat and the other men joined in. The bartender just stood motionless, watching.

But O'Brien had no intention of leaving. Instead, he walked over to the rancher's table and stood in front of him. The hands of the two rannies went out over their guns. But the rancher was relaxed.

'Oh, you want to talk about it?' he asked O'Brien genially. 'I don't talk to buffalo men, boy. Get out of here while you can still leave under your own power.'

In a swift, smooth movement O'Brien swung the muzzle of the long gun up level with the rancher's face; the man was now staring into the barrel of the deadly-looking gun. Both of his rannies drew their weapons. One man was slim and fast, the other one was more clumsy. Both guns were aimed at O'Brien's torso. O'Brien didn't even glance at them.

'You want his head blowed right off his shoulders?' he said quietly.

Behind the long bar the bartender had sucked his breath in and was now holding it, eyes wide.

The rancher, a middle-aged, bony man with dark eyes, looked very different suddenly. He swallowed hard and put a hand up to stop his men.

'Hold it. This boy's got my attention.'

'Put the guns away,' O'Brien said, still focused on the rancher.

The rannies hesitated, but their boss nodded to them. They re-holstered their weapons.

'Now get this,' O'Brien said. 'I never rustled a steer in my life. I ain't responsible for everything some jackass hunter does out there.'

The rancher stared down the barrel of the rifle. O'Brien called to the bartender without looking away.

'Change that order to a dark ale and six boiled eggs.'

The bartender looked at the rancher, then went for the beer.

'And I'd like to eat them eggs in peace,' O'Brien said pointedly.

'I mean, alone.' He dropped the muzzle of the rifle to the floor.

The rancher just sat there for a moment. Then he blew a long breath out and smiled a crooked smile.

'OK, hunter. You made your point.' He rose. 'Come on, boys. The place is his tonight.'

The other men got up, glaring at O'Brien. As the rancher moved past O'Brien he turned to say a last word.

'You got guts, boy. But you better not be here the next time we come in.'

O'Brien just shook his head. Then the rancher and his men left the saloon.

★ ★ ★

A couple of days later, on a warm early-summer night in Billings, Montana McComb and Navarro were in a room that they had at the Langley boarding house just off the main street. McComb had put all the trouble at

Ogallala well out of his mind and was enjoying being back in an area where he had had good times at a younger age.

Billings was on the eastern slopes of the Rocky Mountains. It was a bustling, lively town. Wagons, carriages and buggies rumbled along its broad streets, and women carrying parasols decorated its boardwalks. The Wells Fargo stagecoaches stopped regularly at the largest hotel, and there were several stores on the main street as well as a bank, two other hotels and three saloons. The oldest saloon and the one that McComb sought out immediately upon their arrival, was the Occidental.

The sun was staying up longer now, and there was still light in the western sky when Navarro was looking around in a dry-goods store, hoping to purchase a new vest to replace his worn-out one.

The clerk, a small, bespectacled fellow, had brought out two vests for Navarro to look over. The Mexican held one up now and scowled at it.

'This looks like the cow you took it from pissed on it as a parting *comentario*, my friend. Don't you have something a little more . . . *ranchero*?'

The clerk shrugged. 'I'll take another look out back,' he said testily. Navarro frowned, and drew his Remington Army .44, showing it to the clerk.

'Maybe you don't like serving Mexicanos, heh? Does this give you any more interest?'

The clerk's face went a little pale. 'I'll look real good, mister.'

As the clerk exited the room through a rear door two men walked in from the street. Navarro turned to regard them openly. They walked over to stand beside him at the counter.

'What you buying, Mex?' the closer man asked with a slight grin. 'I don't think they sell them pretty decorated boots in here.'

Navarro stared hard at him. The fellow was rather tall and lanky, with strawlike hair sticking out from under his hat. But the thing that grabbed his attention was his steel nose. Above the nose was one cold-looking eye and one that wandered off to the side. Navarro had heard of such things as the nose but not seen the likes of this.

'*Jesus y Maria,*' Navarro mumbled.

The second man stepped away from the counter so that he could see Navarro better. He was a very thin fellow, an inch or so taller than his comrade, and the lower part of his face was pock-marked heavily. He wore two Wells Fargo revolvers on his belt, a Joslyn .44 in a shoulder holster under his left arm, and a Harrington pocket pistol tucked into his waist at his back. He was Luke 'Iron Kid' Purvis, and was deadly with all the guns.

His odd looking side-kick was Phineas 'No Nose' Foley, and his armor was a Schofield .45 revolver, displayed prominently on his belly.

'What are you saying in Mex, Boy?' Purvis said in a hard, gravelly voice.

'Are you bad-mouthing us in that Mex gibberish?'

Navarro turned to face then warily, displaying his Remington Army .44 so they could see it and how he wore it. He rested his right hand on his belt, just over the gun.

'I can speak English,' he said easily. 'I was just telling myself that your partner there is the ugliest thing I seen since a two-headed calf in Tijuana.'

Foley's bizarre face grew a scowl. 'Why, you damn greaser! Go for your iron.'

But at that moment the clerk returned from the rear. He did not notice the new customers.

'I can't find another vest for you, mister. But I found that shirt that Mr McComb wanted. Oh — I'll be right with you, gentlemen.'

Purvis, the gun-bristling one, put a hand on Foley to slow him down. 'Wait. Did you say McComb?'

'Yes, sir,' the clerk replied.

'Would that be Cyrus McComb?'

Purvis asked eyes narrowed.

'Why, yes. That's his full name, I believe.'

Purvis looked back at Navarro. 'Why would you be picking up something for Cyrus McComb?'

'Because he's my partner,' Navarro said, watching their faces. Purvis took a deep breath in.

'Why, McComb and me go way back, Mex. When he was young and juicy.' He gave a guttural laugh. 'Foley here knows him, too.'

Foley relaxed, and dropped his hand from the Schofield.

'I don't really know him. I met him for five minutes. Years ago.'

'Well, Mex. Any friend of McComb is a friend of mine. I'm the Iron Kid. Made John Wesley Hardin back down once. Last name is Purvis.'

He proffered his hand to Navarro, who hesitated, then took it.

'Luis Navarro. I smoked a pipe with Geronimo once.'

They both grinned.

'I think you're going to work out just fine, Navarro. Now, where can I find my old friend?'

'We're at the boarding house near by.' Navarro told him. Relaxed now. 'But you'll find us at the Occidental just about any evening. I think McComb has the fever for one of the girls there.'

Purvis laughed. No Nose Foley grinned and looked even more grotesque.

'You going to be there tonight?' Foley asked. His steel nose shone in the dim light, and Navarro couldn't help staring. 'I got me a real thirst for that Jamaican rum.'

'We'll probably be there. McComb might have business with you, too.'

'Business?' Purvis queried.

'He's got big plans,' Navarro told him. He glanced at the clerk, who was arranging trousers on a shelf. 'He'll tell you about it.'

Purvis, who did most of the talking for them both, shrugged.

'I'd talk with McComb about most

anything. We'll see you later, then.'

Navarro nodded, and looked over at Foley. 'What happened to your nose, *compadre*?'

Foley frowned. It was a look under which most men would have paled.

'Don't you think maybe that's my business, greaseball?'

Navarro's face went sober. Purvis punched Foley on the arm.

'Hey. This boy is alright, Foley. Go ahead and tell him.'

Foley sighed. 'I met a grizzly on a mountain path. Before I could kill him he'd crushed a rib, scalped me, and bit my nose clean off. They put my scalp back together. But they never found my nose.'

Navarro nodded. 'I knew a man once that lost both eyes to vultures. When he was disabled, you know. They didn't touch him except for his eyes.' He glanced at Foley's left, wandering eye. 'I see you got both of yours.'

Foley gave him a dark look. 'So far.'

Navarro turned to the clerk. 'You can

wrap that shirt up for McComb. I'll go some place else for the vest.' He was gone soon after that.

When he returned to the boarding house, McComb was in their room, oiling his Colt revolver, sitting on a bed. He liked the shirt Navarro brought him. Navarro went to a dry sink, poured some water from a pitcher into a bowl and rinsed his face off.

'I met an old friend of your at the store.'

McComb looked up at him. He looked just as tough and hard as he had at Ogallala, but had a more relaxed manner. He had big plans for himself, and ideas for a new life.

'What old friend?'

'He said his name is Purvis,' Navarro said, towelling his face off. 'He had guns all over him. And he was with the ugliest man I ever seen. *Caramba!* A man with a metal nose, I swear it. And his eyes make you dizzy to look into them. I swear by the Virgin!'

McComb grinned. 'The Iron Kid.

Because he carries so much hardware. That other one is a pinhead named Foley. Purvis introduced us once. I hear he can use a gun, though.'

Navarro came and sat on the other bed, facing him. 'I thought you should see them, Cyrus. Because of what you been talking about.'

McComb raised his eyebrows. 'Hmmph. It's an idea. We can't embark on my new plans with just the two of us. What did you tell them?'

'Just that you might want to talk with them,' Navarro said. 'They said they would be at the Occidental tonight.'

McComb paused, thinking. Then he nodded.

'Good work, *amigo*. This might just be the break we need to start a new life here pronto. I'll see how I react to them. We have to be able to trust them.'

'We will find out tonight,' Navarro said.

A few hours later it was a rather quiet night at the Occidental saloon. It was not a night when the ranch hands came

181

to town, so most patrons were town people of various kinds. Most men wore suits with vests, or dungaree work clothing. Conversation was quiet, and the mood was tranquil. The Occidental management considered their saloon a notch above the other watering holes in town, with its Remington painting behind the bar, potted plants up by the front entrance, and preferred clientele.

When Purvis and Foley walked in through the swinging doors, they looked very much out of place. They had both lived in and around Billings most of their lives, but always frequented the rowdier places. They looked around and saw that McComb and Navarro hadn't arrived yet, so they took a table off in a corner where they could watch the door. A waiter came across with a towel over his arm, and regarded them warily.

'May I help you, gentlemen?' he asked with distain. He took a second look at Foley's nose. Foley looked up at him with the wandering eye.

'There ain't no gentlemen at this table, fruitcake.'

The waiter lost the arrogant look.

'Bring us an unopened bottle of your best rum,' Purvis told him. His pock-marked jaws made his face all bumpy on the lower part. 'And bring four glasses. We're expecting company.'

'Yes, sir.'

'And don't bring no second-rate rum,' Foley said hostilely. 'I want the good Jamaican stuff.'

'We only serve the very best brands of liquors,' the slim young man assured him. 'I'll be right back.'

Purvis looked around the place. 'I ain't been in here for years. I think they went New York on us.'

'I smell ammonia,' Foley complained. He touched his metal nose to settle it in place. It was put on every morning with candle wax.

'I wouldn't never picked this place to meet,' Purvis said. 'But McComb always did have big-city taste. What do you suppose he's got planned for hisself? I know he robbed a couple stages before he decided to actually get a job and work for somebody. I heard it was a hide company.'

Purvis and Foley had also taken part in illicit activities in their past and, since the days when Purvis had known McComb, in this town too. They had recently returned to Billings after enjoying a rather successful period of armed robbery in Utah, where Foley had killed an uncooperative store owner in Provo.

'Only a damn flea-brain would hunt buffalo for a living,' Foley grunted. 'You sure you want to tie up to this bird?'

'McComb ain't no flea-brain,' Purvis told him. 'He was running from something when he done that.' He's got more upstairs than the two of us put together.'

'We'll see,' Foley grunted again, as the waiter delivered their unopened bottle of rum. Foley looked at the label and nodded.

'This is OK.' They were just pouring

the rum when Purvis looked up and saw McComb come through the swinging doors, with Navarro just behind him. Purvis rose.

'McComb! Over here,' he called out, a big grin on his face.

McComb and Navarro arrived at their table. McComb and Purvis embraced for a moment.

'You old scallywag!' Purvis said, grinning. 'I thought I'd never see you again.'

'Well, fate takes its twists and turns,' McComb said, patting Purvis on the shoulder. 'You're looking a little thin, boy. You been riding too hard.'

'I don't stop often enough to eat,' Purvis said. 'This here is a riding partner of mine, Fin Foley. Some folks call him No Nose. Don't pay no attention to his looks. They kind of grow on you.'

McComb went over and shook Foley's hand. 'We met a thousand years ago. Before the nose.'

Foley nodded, looking McComb

over. 'I remember.'

A moment later they were all seated at the table and swigging the rum. After a couple of swigs, McComb turned to Purvis.

'You carry heavy. Can you shoot all them weapons?'

Purvis downed his last swig of rum. 'I've won prizes.'

McComb looked over at Foley. 'Can you shoot straight with that eye?'

Foley's face colored. 'I don't have to prove nothing to you, McComb.'

'Yes you do,' Navarro told him flatly.

Foley gave him a burning look. Purvis caught McComb's gaze.

'He's fast, McComb. Faster than me.'

McComb studied the bizarre face across the table, and finally nodded.

'Sorry about the questions, boys. But this is a kind of interview, you see. I'm going to need a couple of boys that can shoot.'

'Ah,' Purvis said. 'That's what I been thinking.'

'I asked around,' McComb said.

'Before we come over here. I'd guess you two haven't exactly been law-abiding citizens in the past.'

Purvis nodded. 'Maybe.'

'Well, what Navarro and me are planning could get us shot or in prison. Would you be up for that?'

Purvis and Foley exchanged a look. 'Sure,' Purvis finally said. 'What are you thinking about? Stagecoaches?'

McComb looked around them to make sure of privacy. 'No. No stages. No trains. Banks, boys. Just banks.'

'Hmm. Banks,' Purvis mused.

'Banks are where the real money is. And there's no ambushes on the trail, no explosives laid on tracks. You walk in, show your guns, and load up bags with silver and gold.'

'You make it sound real easy,' Foley said acidly. He was slightly retarded and was dull-sounding when he spoke. McComb met his look.

'Sometimes there will be guns. If the feds get involved, there could be ambushes. But the rewards are high, and the doing is simple. All it takes is guts.'

Purvis smiled. 'I thought you liked buffalo hunting.'

McComb made a face. 'That was just a hiatus, a hiding away for a while.' But he thought of Molly, and knew he would have stayed if he could have had Walcott's daughter and, eventually, all that Walcott owned.

'Well, Foley. 'I'm in,' Purvis said. 'What do you say?'

Foley looked from McComb to Navarro. 'For now. Sure.'

'Good,' McComb said. 'Four of us should be just right. Now, there's one thing I want to make clear. I'll be running the show. Any objections to that?'

Purvis and Foley exchanged more looks. 'I reckon that suits us right down to the ground, McComb,' Purvis told him.

'You going after the bank here? The Western Union?' Foley asked. McComb met his dull look impatiently.

'We all live here, Foley. You don't crap in your own bed. No, there's four or five banks worth our attention within a day's ride from here. I been checking that out with locals. My plan is to hit one of them at a time, masked, so they can't trace us back here. When we've got us a big pile, then as our last hit we'll take the Western Union. And then take off for parts unknown. We'll split at that point. Navarro and me will ride south to Mexico. You two can run to your liking.'

Purvis nodded. 'How do you figure a split of the loot?'

McComb took a breath in, and Foley leaned forward on his seat.

'I'll be taking half as my cut,' McComb said deliberately. 'The rest of you will split the other half.'

Foley frowned and looked over at Purvis. 'What the hell!' he complained. McComb narrowed his hard eyes on Foley.

'The whole idea is mine. I'll pick the banks we take. I'll be directing the hold-ups. I'll keep us safe between the jobs. All you'll be doing is pointing your gun at scared tellers and stuffing gold into canvas bags. Now, do you think I deserve less, or you should have more?'

Foley looked down, frowning.

'It's fair, Foley,' Purvis told him quietly. Foley hesitated, then nodded.

'OK. I can do it.'

McComb turned to Navarro, who already knew everything.

'Are we ready to select our first target, then, *compadre*?'

Navarro grinned widely. 'This beats busting our butts for Elias Walcott, *amigo*. A few months from now, we could be richer that him, *si*?'

McComb nodded. 'Exactly. Now, I'll give this some more thought in the next day or two, boys. Then I'll tell you where we'll start our little business. But from now on we should be billeting together.'

'The boarding house would be too public,' Navarro said.

Purvis rubbed his chin. 'We should

have our own place. There's a cabin out on the edge of town. It would be just right. But there's an old man living in it. Used to be a prospector.'

McComb arched his brow. 'Sounds like just what we want.'

'What about the old man?' Foley said.

McComb gave him a look. 'What about him?' He grinned crookedly.

8

O'Brien was still two days' ride from Billings. At the end of a long day of riding he and the appaloosa both needed a rest badly. It was just dusk when he found a suitable campsite where a small creek would provide water for both of them. When he picketed the mount to a cottonwood sapling near the water it guffered at him. He touched its flank. He was becoming fond of the horse.

'I get it. You're glad the day's over. Me too.'

He watered and fed the appaloosa before he did anything for himself. Then he cleared a space from leaves a small distance from the stream. He laid down a buffalo robe from his bedroll, as a ground sheet, before putting his bedroll down. After gathering some firewood, he started a fire with a chunk of flint and his Bowie. Soon he had the flames crackling in the growing dark. He was preparing to fry up an antelope steak in a small pan when he heard the sound in the creek. There was a dull splashing of water, then another sound, a grunting noise, and he recognized it immediately.

In the next moment a grizzly bear, one of the biggest he had ever seen, came splashing out of the water. It leapt onto the side of the appaloosa, which whinnied and bucked to avoid the attack.

O'Brien swore loudly. Both he and the horse had been distracted by their food and had missed the smell of the bear as it approached across the water. O'Brien's rifles were still on the appaloosa's irons.

The bear raked long claws across the horse's flank, trying to bring it down, but the big stallion turned and bucked. It smashed a hoof into the grizzly's chest, busting a rib and throwing the bear onto its back. Then the horse broke free of its tether and ran off into the darkness.

The bear regained its feet, turned slightly, and remembered O'Brien. He was a second choice, but good enough. It felt some pain in its side, but it wasn't enough to slow it down. It rose up on its hind legs and roared out its warning to him. It meant business. O'Brien would be its next meal.

The fire was still between them, and the bear began circling around it. It was obviously afraid of the fire, but only minimally.

The only weapon O'Brien had was the skinning knife on his right boot, but it was not much against a half-ton of bear. That would be his last resort.

The bear came around the fire to his right; the look in its eyes was deadly. There was no point in running: the bear could run faster. And it could climb trees better than he could. There was little choice. He had to stand and fight.

He had killed his first bear when he was very young, but it wasn't a grizzly.

He remembered his Scots father telling him that if you're caught without a gun when a bear comes, there's one thing left to do. Improvise.

He looked down at the fire as the bear came around it, and picked up a thick piece of firewood only burning on one end. The bear was moving toward him, just fifteen feet away. It stopped when it saw the firebrand and roared angrily at him.

Instead of backing up O'Brien yelled out a growling roar of his own, and waved the firebrand. It burned wildly, and made kaleidoscopic patterns of light across the darkness.

The bear was impressed, but not cowed. It rose up on its hind legs again, and roared its blood-chilling message into the blackness. In that moment O'Brien took a big chance: he gave up his weapon by hurling it at the bear's chest.

What he hoped would happen, did. The fire caught the bear's chest and forelegs and took hold of him. In just a half-second the animal was ablaze along its front. It swiped at the flame, and then went back down on all fours, turned and ran for the creek. The fire was extinguished there, but the bear didn't even look back. It kept running off into the trees.

O'Brien slumped onto the ground. He had been lucky. He couldn't have counted on the knife. His father had also told him once that a bear isn't dead until you get it skinned and the hide cured.

It took him most of an hour to find the appaloosa. It was downstream a half-mile, skitter and jumpy. It was glad to see him.

'All right, I know. Here. Let me see that.'

There were two long gashes in its flank, on the left, but they weren't very deep.

'Hell, you're all right. I been scratched worse than that with prickly pear. I'll rub some grease on that, I won't tell you what kind or you'd run another mile. Come on, you'll be ready to ride at sunup.'

It was another hour before he had the steak on the fire and the appaloosa was settled down near by. This time his saddle supported him on the ground, and his rifles were beside him on his groundsheet. He had dressed the appaloosa's wounds with bear grease, and it seemed comfortable now. You never knew what little surprises you might get out on the trail, and maybe that was what he had begun liking about it.

He had two corn dodgers with the steak, and real coffee, which was more expensive than chicory. When he had cleaned up after himself he sat on his saddle and let thoughts fly through his head like bats in a cave. He had no good evidence that McComb had actually ended up in Billings, or even Montana. He had no idea at this point how much time it would take to find him. But he knew that he would keep looking, no matter how long it took.

Somebody had to take McComb down. He was a killer, and it appeared that O'Brien was the only one with the motivation to stop him.

He scented the air for a moment, he could smell things other men couldn't, and Wells Fargo drivers told it around that he could hear a man's arm swinging in its socket at a hundred yards in a windstorm. O'Brien only shook his head at such stories, but no man had ever drawn on him from behind when he hadn't heard it in time to react.

He sniffed again; there was no scent of the bear coming back at them. The fight with O'Brien had probably been its only real experience of fire.

Molly Walcott, he mused now, was probably sitting on her front porch with Matt Dawkins, firming up wedding plans. The boy had been brash as a flour peddler running for governor in his pursuit of the boss's daughter. But it had all paid off when two of her wooers had abandoned their suits. Persistence pays, O'Brien thought, sitting there poking at his fire. It was a lesson not to be lost on him.

Actually, he had misgivings about Molly. What man, he thought, wouldn't want Molly to cuddle up to on a cold winter night, or to fry his eggs for him in the morning. A small part of him felt he had been a little loco in pushing her away. But the bigger part, the part that determined who he really was, told him that he had to school himself on the trail, and know the great wilderness around him as well as Chief Gray Hawk. He sensed that there was an adventure out there, just waiting for him, experiences that would make him into a mature man. He could not give all that up at this age to tie himself to a life of domesticity and predictability. It was something in his blood, something that had brought his Highlander Scots father over the sea to a new world, escaping from some indiscretion he had never talked about.

'But I do miss you, Molly,' he said

aloud to the fire. Then he thrust a stick rather fiercely into its flames.

The rest of that night was uneventful. He awoke to a red-streaked sky and a wide-awake stallion, which nickered at him when it saw him stir.

'OK. I'm up,' he replied.

He went and examined the horse's wounds and applied a new layer of bear grease. The horse shied slightly when the grease was applied, and a muscle in its flank twitched. But then it settled down.

'That ain't what you think,' O'Brien lied.

Within an hour they were under way again. O'Brien rode hard all morning, and paused just briefly under a plane tree to down a muffin dry. He didn't like to waste any time because he had no idea how long McComb would be in Billings even if he was there.

He rode steadily that afternoon, thinking about McComb. Thinking he had to uncover more evidence that he was on the right trail to eventually confront that killer.

He had killed twice already in his young life, but always to defend his own life. He had never gone after a man to seek retribution for a wrong already done. He had no interest in enforcing the law, though, or in arresting McComb. He was going after him to make it right for Uriah Cahill, O'Brien's hunting partner. The man whose life he had saved from wolves. The fellow who had been going to teach O'Brien to read.

He was going to Billings to kill.

In late afternoon, O'Brien crested a ridge and saw a small cabin set in hilly terrain, with smoke lofting from its chimney. He looked around, there was no horse in sight. The doorway was slightly open.

'Let's check it out,' he said to the horse.

He reigned in just outside the cabin, dismounted, and picketed his mount to the ground. He walked around the back of the small structure; there was no horse there, either.

He came round to the front again and looked past a leather-hinged oak door into the cabin. 'Hello! Anybody here?'

Silence.

He stepped inside. There was nobody there. A fire burned low in a fireplace on his left. There was a double bunk in a corner, a crude table, and two straight-backed chairs. An empty bottle of whiskey stood on the table, and there were scraps of hardtack on a tin plate.

'Well,' he mumbled, 'I'll get nothing on McComb here.'

The unwritten law in the wild was that a traveller might help himself to another man's coffee in the owner's absence. So O'Brien, seeing a pot of coffee hanging over the fire on a hook, took it off and poured himself a half-cup of the warm liquid. He was just taking his second sip when he heard a sound outside. His movement at the fire had obliterated any earlier sounds.

He turned with the cup still in his hand, and saw a wild-looking man come through the door, followed by a second one. They were brothers, and trappers. The first one wore no hat and his hair was wild and long. His cheeks were sallow on a wind-burned face. His brother was a bit taller and had an ugly burn mark all across the left side of his face.

The first brother raised a Remington shotgun to O'Brien's chest level. His hard eyes narrowed down to slits.

'What the hell you think you're doing, mister?'

O'Brien sighed. If it wasn't bears it was half-wit strangers.

'Just having a cup of your coffee, till you got back,' he answered, eyeing the cannon-like shotgun. His rifles were still on the appaloosa. 'I wanted to ask about a couple of men.'

The second brother came around to get a better look at O'Brien.

'What are you? A goddam buffalo-hunter?'

O'Brien hesitated. Yes.'

'Tie him up, Lem,' the first one said, holding the gun steady on O'Brien.

O'Brien frowned. 'Look, you see I'm unarmed. I didn't come in here to cause trouble. I'll just be on my way.'

'You aint going nowhere, rawhide,' Lem told him. He retrieved a length of rope from a wall nail and went over to O'Brien.

O'Brien's first impulse was to send Lem across the room with one punch. But then he was likely to be torn literally in half by the shotgun. So he let the scarred man push him onto a chair and tie his wrists behind him while his mind worked on alternative defences.

'He's tied, Zeb,' Lem told his brother.

'What's the matter with you two?' O'Brien said in a low voice. 'I can pay you for the coffee.'

Zeb with the shotgun learned over O'Brien. 'It ain't about the coffee. It's about our space, buffalo man. You boys think the whole damn country is yours to use like you want. This here is our cabin, and you violated it. You got to pay.'

'You got to pay!' Lem said in a shriller voice.

With no warning Zeb swung the barrel on the long gun at O'Brien's head. O'Brien tried to duck away, but it cracked up loudly beside his right ear. He almost fell off the chair and bright colored lights flashed on in his skull. He gasped out in pain. Blood ran down onto his neck.

Both brothers were laughing.

'What do you think of that, hunter?' Lem squealed.

O'Brien looked up, his eyes had changed. A wide grin slid off Lem's scarred face.

'You boys are making are big mistake,' O'Brien growled.

More laughter, mostly by Zeb. 'That's just the start of it, mister. You'll be a couple hours entertainment before it's over for you.'

Lem was angry inside because

O'Brien's look had scared him. He got an idea that appealed to him.

'Hey. We still got that branding-iron you found near that ranch a few weeks ago?'

O'Brien had held his wrists just apart when Lem had bound his hands, and now was working with the ropes as the two men talked. If he worked loose, he hoped a situation would occur when they would be separated momentarily. They both wore sidearms.

'Oh, I think I threw it out back somewhere,' Zeb now replied.

'Well don't you think that might liven the evening up some?' Lem said meaningfully. 'We got a good fire going over there.'

O'Brien worked carefully at the rope. He couldn't move much or they would figure out what he was doing, and it would be all over. Maybe permanently.

Zeb's face broke into a nasty grin. 'I see where you're headed,' he said. 'We could take that rawhide off his chest and have us a little buffalo boy roast.'

Lem nodded vigorously. 'That what I thought.'

'Go find that iron out there and bring it in,' Zeb said still grinning. 'We could make this last all evening. I'll keep this shotgun on him till you get back.'

O'Brien had already loosened the rope enough to slide one hand free. As Zeb watched his brother leave he pulled the rope unobtrusively off the other hand. It hit the seat of the chair behind him but made no noise. Now was the time. This would probably be the only moment all evening when the brothers would be separated.

Zeb sat down on a chair across the table from O'Brien, the shotgun still aimed at O'Brien's chest. The slightest wrong move by O'Brien would result in his belly being blown out through his back.

'Well, buffalo man. You ready for a little branding? I hear enough of them irons on you will send your whole body into shock, so we'll have to go real slow with you. You know, to keep you alive.

We don't want you slipping away on us. He turned slightly on the chair. 'Lem! Get in here with that iron.'

In that split second O'Brien's hands came forward and lifted the table up violently, throwing it against Zeb. The double-barrel Remington roared in the small space, making O'Brien's ears ring so loudly all other sound was obliterated. The shot took a half-moon chunk out of the top edge of the table, and blasted a hole in the roof a man's head could have poked through.

O'Brien drew the Bowie from his stovepipe boot then and threw himself wildly between the upright legs of the table. Zeb was still grabbing the shotgun, but it was useless now. When O'Brien landed on him he drove the knife into Zeb's chest up to the hilt.

Zeb's eyes saucered, then a puzzled frown came onto his ugly face, as if he didn't quite understand what had happened.

In the next moment Lem appeared big-eyed in the open doorway, the branding-iron in one hand and a Schofield revolver in the other. He took one quick look and aimed the gun at O'Brien's face.

But O'Brien had picked up the shotgun from the floor, and just in that half-second in eternity he squeezed its trigger and beat Lem to the draw. Another blast roared deafeningly in the cabin, and the shot hit Lem in his midriff, almost cutting him in half. He went flying back through the doorway and landed dead, outside in the growing darkness.

O'Brien walked out and looked at the corpse. It was a bloody mess. He came back in, set the shotgun aside, and looked down at Zeb. He had died when the big Bowie found his heart.

'I tried to tell you, you jackass,' O'Brien growled down at him.

The appaloosa guffered outside, jerking on its tether. One of the brothers' mounts had broken loose and run. O'Brien could barely hear the appaloosa, with his ears still ringing.

He looked around the cabin. He found an unopened tin of pears on a shelf, and looked for something to open it with. He stepped over and around the corpse of Zeb on the floor. He turned the table back up, sat down at it, and ate the pears slowly. They tasted good, and he had earned them.

When he left shortly afterwards, he didn't even glance at Lem's corpse out by the horses. He took the saddle off the other horse, threw it onto the ground, and slapped the animal on the rump. It ran off into the night. Then he boarded the appaloosa. It was spooked.

'Everything's just fine,' he told it, patting its neck. Then he rode off to find a campsite for the night.

It had been another eventful day on the trail.

9

That next day in Ogallala was a gala day.

Molly Walcott and Matt Dawkins were married at the local church with a full, formal ceremony. Dawkins wore a jacket and a lariat tie, and with his hair slicked back and a clean shave he gave the appearance of a rather handsome groom. Molly wore a white satin dress and veil, and with her blonde hair she caused some gasps of appreciation as she came up the aisle with her father.

At the reception in Walcott's back garden all the young men who had been would be suitors of Molly got to kiss her at last as Dawkins's bride, not wanting to miss the opportunity. There was a steak fry, and liquor for the men, and an elderly man played a violin off in a corner.

Dawkins felt very smug. Almost every

bachelor in town envied him. Midway through the festivities, when he was standing off to one side with his arm around his new wife, Walcott walked over to them, holding a glass of ale.

'Well. The newlyweds seem to be surviving the hoopla. Can I get you anything, Matt?'

Proud-looking, gangly Matt grinned broadly. 'No, sir. I got all I want. Right here beside me.'

Molly looked up at him and smiled. She was happy. She was about to take her place in Ogallala society as one of its influential matrons, and she liked the idea. She looked beautiful, standing there in her wedding dress. She had liked being the centre of attention today, and all week. Being married gave her sudden importance in her family, and in the town.

'So have I.' She returned the compliment. She turned to Walcott. 'Oh. You said you had another gift for us, Daddy.'

'That's just why I came over here to

find you,' Walcott said. He looked over at Dawkins. 'Matt, as you know, I haven't chosen a new foreman for my hunting crew since McComb rode out.'

'Yes, sir. I know.'

'Well, Matt, I want you to be my new foreman,' Walcott grinned at him. 'And that's my other wedding present to you both.'

They were both smiling widely. 'Oh, Daddy!' Molly cried out. She hugged him and almost knocked the ale from his hand.

'I don't know what to say,' Dawkins stammered. 'I ain't one of the old-timers here, sir.'

'No, but you got a good head on your shoulders,' Walcott told him. 'And you're married to my daughter. You have to be a man respected by the community. The job is yours.'

'Thank you, sir. It looks like McComb did me a big favour.'

And O'Brien, Walcott thought to himself.

'I wonder if he really headed out to

Montana?' Dawkins mused.

'And if O'Brien is out there looking for him,' Walcott said soberly.

Molly's expression fell into straight lines, the blush of gaiety leaving it momentarily. She turned without thinking and looked out toward the west. Both Walcott and Dawkins noticed. Walcott spoke to Dawkins.

'She prays for him regular,' he told the young groom. 'O'Brien. They were good friends, you know.'

Molly turned back to them. 'Yes,' she said. 'Just good friends.' Then she brightened her face and took Dawkins' arm. 'Come on, new husband. Our guests will be missing us.'

★ ★ ★

On that same afternoon, in a small town a half-day's ride from Billings, McComb and his small gang rode in quietly and reined up at the local bank. The foursome just sat their mounts for a long moment, looking the place over.

214

McComb finally turned to the others.

'It's perfect. Small. No guards, I'm told. And they got a shipment of silver in just days ago. What do you think, boys? It's there for the taking.'

'I say we should get at it,' Navarro replied, grinning.

'Let's do it,' Purvis added.

Foley, with the steel nose and wandering eye, growled and dismounted with them. Foley was disgruntled with the world in general, and he was hoping for some action inside the bank, as well as the silver.

With their mounts all tethered outside, there were two teller windows, but no other customers in the place. On the way in the four had pulled the woollen masks over their faces. There was just one teller at his window, and when he saw the masks he let out a small cry. A woman clerk at a desk behind him looked up and screamed. There were two other persons back there, both men. One looked like the manager.

'All right, keep the noise down,' McComb barked out. 'This is a hold-up, and we came for money. Not to hurt anybody. You do what you're told and you'll live through this.'

'Please, mister,' the teller said through a suddenly dry mouth. 'Don't shoot anybody.'

The manager stood up, back at an oak desk. He was heavyset and partially bald.

'There's nothing for you here, boys. We're low on cash ourselves. You can have what's in the tellers' drawers up there.'

McComb turned to Navarro and Purvis. 'Go empty them drawers,' he told them. Then he turned to Foley. 'You stay here and watch for trouble.'

Foley nodded behind the mask.

McComb, Navarro and Purvis went through a gate in the barrier. While the other two were helping themselves to cash at the windows, McComb went back to the manager.

'Is that the safe back there?' McComb said.

'Yes, sir. But there isn't much there. Stocks and bonds you can't cash. Legal papers.'

'What about the silver that was just delivered to you a couple days ago?' McComb growled out. The manager swallowed hard.

'Oh, that's all paid out. We move the cash in and out here pretty fast.'

'Go open the damn safe,' McComb said.

'But I just told you.'

McComb slammed the barrel of his Colt against the manager's head, and the fellow saw colored lights for a moment as he fell against the desk. He was gasping wheezily.

'Maybe I didn't make myself clear,' McComb said in a hard voice. 'The safe.'

The manager staggered over to the safe, dialed a combination lock for a moment, then swung the heavy door open. McComb walked up to it and saw the sacks of silver on a wide shelf. He turned to the others.

'Get over here. We got silver to haul out.'

'Don't take it all, mister,' the manager begged, holding his head. 'The ranchers around here will kill me.'

McComb was tired of him. He levelled the Colt at his face and fired. The manager was thrown back against the vault door, a hole over his left eye. When he slid to the floor, he left a crimson stain on the door.

'That's for lying to us,' McComb grumbled.

The woman started screaming again and McComb aimed the gun at her.

'I told you, lady. Keep it quiet and you live.'

Her screams subdued to a whimper as Navarro and Purvis hauled the sacks past McComb. McComb grabbed one that was left, and they all headed back out. As they came beyond the barrier an old man walked in the door. He stared at them, wide-eyed.

The three carrying sacks ahead of McComb came past him with barely a glance, but as McComb passed him he gave the gray-haired fellow a violent shove aside, knocking him down. He hit the floor hard and lay there, stunned.

'You goddam lowlifes!' he choked out. 'You can't get away with this! You'll all fry in hell!'

Foley turned back. He drew his Schofield casually and fired it three times into the old man's chest. His body jerked with each shot, then he lay bloody and lifeless. The woman behind the barrier began screaming yet again, but she was safe now. The other three with the loot were already boarding their mounts outside, and Foley was on his way out the door.

Moments later the four riders were gone from the small town and on their way back to Billings. There was no law to follow them, and nobody knew what they looked like.

It had been a successful foray into a

new life for them, and McComb was very pleased.

A few hours later they were back at the cabin outside town. On the previous day they had shot the old prospector who owned it and buried him out in back of the cabin. McComb dumped all the silver and paper money onto a table in the centre of the cabin and all four of them looked down on the loot with greedy eyes.

'That is more than we thought, *compadre*,' Navarro said grinning past a dark mustache. He picked up a handful of coins and let them fall through his fingers.

'This is just the beginning,' McComb told them. 'Just the beginning.'

'When do we split up?' Foley said petulantly.

His sidekick Purvis, still bristling with his guns, turned to him.

'We'll all get our cut, partner. Be patient.'

'Part of it's mine,' Foley said in his dull voice.

'I haven't forgotten that,' McComb told him acidly. 'Well divide it up tonight. Tomorrow we'll start thinking about another bank in a little place south of here. No law there, either.' He added this last, with satisfaction. Navarro looked over at him.

'You know, *amigo*, every time we do this, we draw more interest from the authorities. Those two we shot back there. That could bring in a federal marshal.'

McComb frowned at his old partner. 'What are you saying? That I shouldn't've shot that lying sonofabitch manager?'

Navarro shook his head. 'I'm just pointing out that every time we do one of these lesser banks, we increase the risk to ourselves, yes?'

'You want to just leave it all laying in them vaults, waiting for somebody else to come and help hisself to it?'

Navarro shrugged. 'We could go directly for the big bank right here next. The Western Union. They probably

221

have enough to make us all rich in just one more job.'

McComb sat down on a chair. It wasn't a bad idea. He looked over to Purvis.

'What do you think?' he asked him.

'I kind of like it, McComb,' the Iron Kid said thoughtfully.

'Yeah,' Foley said, bright-eyed. 'The big bank next.'

McComb pursed his lips. 'That ain't bad thinking, *amigo*. This one got us more than I thought. The Western Union could be very big.'

Navarro nodded. 'Just as important, we can all ride out from here right after the big job. Even if marshals are brought in, we'll be halfway to Mexico before they even begin looking. And they won't know who to go after, anyway.'

McComb nodded. 'OK. I like it. And we won't wait for this job today to get old on us. I'll start working on it tonight. We ought to be able to do it by, say, day after tomorrow. Then we can say goodbye to Billings for ever. I never really liked the place, anyway.'

Purvis nodded. 'Then it's agreed. The Western Union, and then we're gone.'

'Gone,' Foley said rather too loudly.

'Let's put this stuff away and go celebrate,' said McComb. He grinned.

★   ★   ★

One hour after that conversation at the prospector's shack O'Brien rode into town.

He looked the place over as he traversed the main street, and was impressed. It was more civilized than he was accustomed to. He stopped at the Occidental saloon, hitched the appaloosa outside, and went in.

It was late afternoon and there were few customers. O'Brien was impressed with the grandeur of the place. He felt as if he were in Kansas City. McComb and his men hadn't arrived yet.

He went to the long bar and

addressed a slim, clean-looking bartender.

'You got quite a place here.'

The bartender looked him over disdainfully.

'What can I get you, sir?'

'Make it a double whiskey,' O'Brien told him.

'Any particular brand?'

O'Brien shook his head. 'But maybe you can help me with some information. I'm looking for a rough-looking *hombre* with a scar on the side of his face. He goes by the name of McComb. He might have a Mexican with him.'

'We're not supposed to talk about our customers,' the fellow said,

O'Brien took a double eagle from a leather poke and threw it onto the bar.

'That's for the drink. And for what you know.'

The barkeep surreptitiously took the gold coin, and leaned forward toward O'Brien.

'He's been in here several times. With a Mexican. The last time he was with two other men, too.'

'Two other men?'

'They were bad looking fellows. One had a metal nose. I was afraid he would scare our other customers away.'

O'Brien thought about that for a moment.

'What time do they usually come in?'

'If they come in it will be later,' was the reply.

'Do you know where they sleep?'

The fellow shook his head. 'But the Langley boarding house is just on the next street. You might try there.'

O'Brien threw another coin onto the bar.

'You been a big help.'

After his drink O'Brien walked his mount over to the boarding house near by. It looked a lot like Elias Walcott's house in Ogallala. He mounted some steps and walked into the carpeted parlor.

He filled the doorway with his distinctive silhouette. He held his Winchester loosely under his right arm.

When he walked over to a registration desk his spurs made rhythmic metallic sounds in the silence of the big room. A slim young man in Eastern clothing took a look at him, rose from a chair, and hastily exited the parlor.

There was a man behind the desk with a green visor on his head and a deep frown as he read the page of a local newspaper. When he looked up at O'Brien, he jumped slightly. Then looked him over warily.

'May I help you?'

'I guess you rent rooms,' O'Brien said.

The man reluctantly nodded. A sigh.

'Yes. We do.'

'I might want one later.'

'Yes. Of course.' Stiffly.

'In the meantime, do you have a guest here by the name of McComb?'

'Why, no, we don't. But he was here. With another man.'

'A Mexican?'

The fellow nodded, making a face.

'Yes. A Mexican. Are you a friend?'

O'Brien scowled at him, making the fellow lick dry lips.

'So they moved out?'

A nod. 'Just recently.'

'Do you know where they went?'

The clerk hesitated. Then, 'Not really.'

O'Brien could see in the man's eyes that he knew something. He leaned forward onto the desk.

'Do you really want to lie to me?' he said in a brittle tone.

The clerk wilted under the look.

'Well, they did mention some cabin they were going to move into.'

'What cabin? Where?'

'I honestly don't know.' Fearfully.

O'Brien went outside to think things over, standing beside his horse. He had always known he might have to go through Navarro to get to McComb. He felt the Mexican was almost as culpable as McComb, anyway, in Cahill's killing. But now there were others whom McComb had gathered to him and undoubtedly they would defend him, just as Navarro would.

Well, he thought, if the last two keep out of my way, they'll live. If they don't, they won't. It is that simple for them.

He decided he wouldn't look for the cabin. Not yet. He was sure that if he visited the Occidental every night he would run into some or all of them. He would play the cards dealt him at that time.

He had no idea that in two days McComb would be gone from Billings. For ever.

He billeted the appaloosa at a nearby hostelry that afternoon, stopped in at the Occidental briefly without seeing McComb or any of the others, then he returned to the boarding house. The same clerk was on duty inside, and was obviously sorry to see O'Brien back.

'Yes, sir. We have a room for you,' he told O'Brien. He looked down at the Winchester under O'Brien's arm. 'You taking that in with you?'

O'Brien gave him a withering look.

'Just tell me what room.'

The clerk's smile faded. 'Yes, sir. Here's the key to 206.'

O'Brien took it. 'Don't mention I'm here to anybody. You understand?'

The clerk looked scared again. 'Well, some ugly-looking man came in here just after you left earlier. Wore one of those metal noses. He hadn't applied it well, and it looked like it would fall off at any minute. It makes you sick.'

O'Brien was frowning impatiently.

'You told him about me?'

'He was here to get a skinning knife Mr McComb left in his room. I might have mentioned you were asking about McComb.'

O'Brien looked away, digesting that. The clerk tried a smile.

'Sorry. I told him I didn't know your name. I just said you were wearing rawhides.' O'Brien let a long breath out.

'Now they know.'

'I thought they were your friends.'

'You ought to get out from behind that counter and learn about the real world,' O'Brien said sourly. Then he went up to his room.

Things were radically different now. The element of surprise would be gone. McComb would be prepared for him. Waiting. With four guns to defend him, he figured.

But circumstances dictated that McComb would not know he was there. Not yet. Before returning to the cabin with McComb's knife, No Nose Foley elected to visit the Occidental for a quick beer. When he got there he found Navarro sitting alone with a bottle of tequila before him.

'Hey, Mex! I though you was back at the cabin?'

Navarro regarded him balefully. He had never liked Foley from the time they were introduced.

'Oh, Foley. You're supposed to be back there chopping firewood.'

Foley came and sat down and took a swig out of Navarro's bottle, uninvited.

Navarro looked at Foley's maladjusted nose and shook his head. Foley didn't see the gesture.

'McComb sent me to get his knife. He left it at the boarding house,' Foley explained. He leaned forward confidentially. 'I got some news.'

Navarro narrowed his dark eyes on him.

'News?'

'Somebody come looking for McComb.'

Navarro set his glass down.

'What? Where?'

'There at the boarding house. Just today.'

All sounds in the saloon were suddenly closed off to Navarro's hearing.

'Did you find out what this man looks like?'

Foley grinned. 'Sure I asked. What do you think?'

'Well?' Navarro said impatiently.

'He was tall. Big. Wearing rawhides.'

Navarro felt his stomach lurch.

'*Jesus y Maria!*' he whispered.

Foley frowned. 'What's the matter? Maybe he's one of McComb's old friends.'

231

Navarro wasn't listening. It had to be O'Brien. He had come to avenge Cahill's murder. And if he had come this far for McComb, he was here with deadly resolve.

'We got to get back to the cabin,' he said thickly. He poured himself a last drink and swigged it down.

As he put his glass back down, O'Brien walked through the swinging doors. The Winchester was nestling snugly under his arm.

Navarro saw him immediately.

O'Brien scanned the room. His eyes fell on Navarro. He just stood there for a moment, attracting some attention from nearby tables. He looked big, primitive and dangerous.

'*Dios mio!*' Navarro muttered. He looked over at Foley. 'Are you as fast with that Schofield as Purvis claims you are?'

Foley frowned. 'You want to try me?'

Navarro motioned to O'Brien. 'No. But he might.'

Foley turned and saw O'Brien. 'Oh.

The rawhide man.'

'And he's no friend of McComb,' Navarro said as O'Brien started toward them.

Foley grinned an ugly grin. 'Well, then let's kill him.'

O'Brien stopped a few feet away from their table.

'Where's McComb, Navarro?' he said in a deep growl.

Navarro found his courage.

'Are you loco, rawhide? It is not just McComb now. It is all four of us. Can you go up against that?'

O'Brien took a breath in. 'I don't have to go up against all of you,' he corrected him. 'I found you, Navarro. That's good enough for now.'

Navarro could feel his heart pummelling his chest. He knew how good O'Brien was with a rifle, and he had heard stories about him. Stories he had never believed. Until now.

'I didn't kill Cahill. Your beef is with McComb. And he'll find you before you find him.'

'You got to answer for Cahill, too,' O'Brien said. 'Every ugly thought he had, you had. You was right beside him, telling him to do it. You're going down.'

Navarro and Foley rose from the table. They both faced O'Brien. Suddenly the entire saloon was deathly quiet. Two men sitting behind Navarro's table got up and moved into a far corner. A heavy bartender stopped his work and saw what was happening.

'Hey, boys! We don't allow any gunplay inside here. Take it out on the street.'

'Shut up,' O'Brien growled out without looking at him.

Foley couldn't see what all the fuss was about. He turned to Navarro.

'Leave this to me. I'll put three in him while he's figuring it all out.'

In the next moment he drew the Schofield so fast the eye couldn't follow.

But O'Brien, who was accustomed to watch the eyes of men and animals alike to access next moves, had seen Foley's good eye squint down almost invisibly just before he went for iron. In that half-instant, O'Brien fell into a low crouch, and when Foley's gun roared in the room, its hot lead hit O'Brien in the left arm instead of his chest. Between that shot and Navarro's drawing, O'Brien staggered backward a step, then fired off a quick round at Foley.

The rifle roared out even louder than the revolver of Foley, and Foley was struck in center chest, flying off his feet like a circus aerialist and crashing into two tables before hitting the floor, eyes wide in the rictus of death.

Navarro's Remington Army .44 blasted out its retort as Foley was blown off his feet. O'Brien's turn toward him had partially ruined Navarro's aim, and his shot had just grazed O'Brien's right side as he fired off a second round from the big gun that hit Navarro in the gut. O'Brien fired yet again and struck the Mexican just between the eyes, sending him plummeting to the floor. He was dead before he hit. He made the floor shake and the crotch of his trousers went damp.

The air was so thick with gunsmoke that it penetrated customers' nostrils and left an iron taste in the mouth.

O'Brien levered the rifle again in a swift, smooth action, and glanced down at Navarro. There was no movement. Nobody in the room broke the new silence. Nobody moved. O'Brien, looking even more dangerous now, walked over to Foley and stood over him.

Foley was a grotesque sight. His wandering eye, still open, was looking in a different direction from the up-staring one. His metal nose had been knocked off, revealing a scarred hole in Foley's face.

'That's the ugliest thing I ever looked on,' O'Brien said casually. He looked as unruffled as when he had walked in. His blood pressure had not even risen above normal. He walked over to the bar and threw a gold coin on it. 'That's for their drinks, and for the clean-up,' he said acidly. He was frustrated because he still hadn't found McComb and he was bleeding from his arm and side.

As he walked to the front doors two men at the bar stumbled quickly out of his path, almost knocking each other over. As he left he punched an elbow into one of the swinging doors, causing three slats to fall out.

Nobody protested about the manner of his exit.

10

O'Brien spent most of the next hour in a doctor's office down at the end of the street.

The silver-haired medic just put salve on the shallow side wound, but had to apply a thick bandage to O'Brien's left arm. When he was finished he went over to a counter and got a length of cloth from a drawer.

'I'll have to put a sling on that arm. It should only take a few minutes.'

O'Brien shook his head. Sitting here with his rawhide shirt off, he looked very muscular and athletic. Very primitive. He already had two thick scars on his torso.

'Don't bother, Doc.'

The doctor turned to him with a frown. O'Brien was gingerly moving the arm, testing it. His face didn't react to the pain. The doctor shook his head.

'Are you immune to pain, boy?'

'I just don't pay no attention to it,' O'Brien told him.

'Well, at least take a bottle of laudanum with you.'

O'Brien gave him a tired smile 'Just tell me what I owe you, Doc, and I'll be out of here.' He was pulling the tunic back on carefully, over the bandage.

'Well, suit yourself. But if I was you I'd take a little more interest in my own welfare.'

O'Brien caught his gaze. 'If you was me, Doc, you'd be dead now.'

The doctor frowned quizzically at him for a moment. Then he went to write up a bill for him.

Down at the Occidental McComb and Purvis had just walked into the saloon looking for Navarro and Foley. They were surprised not to find them there. McComb walked over to the bartender.

'We're looking for a couple of friends. They was with us when we was in here before. You seen them?'

The bartender's eyes widened slightly.

'Oh, yes. I remember you were in here together.' He took a long breath in. 'Well. You missed all the excitement. Those two were just hauled down to the morgue, mister.'

McComb looked at him as if he had gone crazy.

'The morgue? What the hell are you saying? We must be talking about different men.'

'No, sir. These were the ones you were drinking with. A Mexican and that weird-looking fellow. With the nose.'

Purvis had come up beside McComb and they now turned to each other with stunned looks. McComb turned back to the barkeep.

'They're dead?'

A casual nod. 'Yep. Had the biggest gunfight in here ever saw. Some big man wearing rawhides. The nose man tried to kill him when he came in. But it didn't work out that way. I've never seen anybody that good with a rifle.'

McComb looked down at the bar. 'O'Brien.'

'Who?' Purvis frowned.

'I told the sheriff,' the bartender went on, 'that they drew on him. He won't even be questioned.'

McComb couldn't focus his thoughts. He glanced over at Purvis.

'Some punk kid from Nebraska. We hunted buffalo together.'

'What the hell would he have against Navarro?' Purvis said. 'And Foley?'

'Nothing, really,' McComb heard himself saying, as if through a long tube. 'It's me he really wants.'

Purvis was still frowning.

'Did you two have a spat back there?' asked the bartender with a smile.

McComb turned suddenly and headed for the door. Purvis hesitated, then followed him. Out beside their mounts, McComb turned to him.

'I can't just wait for him to find me. I got to find him. Maybe surprise him. This boy is dangerous.'

'Obviously,' the Iron Kid said. All

four of his guns were visible on him, and he instinctively put his right hand over one of the Wells Fargo revolvers on his hip. 'I can't even imagine how he took Foley down.'

'We're making a stop at the boarding house,' McComb told him.

A few minutes later they were standing in the carpeted parlor talking to the clerk you had checked O'Brien in.

'Oh, Mr McComb, isn't it? Can I rent you another room, gentlemen?

'We ain't here for a room,' McComb grated out. He was still very upset. Not only was his life in danger, but O'Brien had fouled up all his plans to get rich quick. 'Has a big man in rawhides checked in here?'

The clerk's mind raced back to O'Brien's warning. Not to mention his residence there to anybody. O'Brien had impressed the clerk that bad things would result from his violation of that prohibition.

'Why, let's see. A man in rawhides.

No, I guess not. I haven't seen anybody of that description.'

McComb drew his Colt and showed it to the clerk.

'Are you sure?'

The clerk felt his stomach contract. But it was too late now to admit he had lied.

'Yes, sir. I'm quite sure.'

McComb holstered the gun. 'I better not find out otherwise,' he spat out. Then he and Purvis left the place.

Outside, as they untethered their mounts, Purvis turned to McComb.

'Look, whoever this O'Brien is, why should we worry about it? There's two of us with fast guns. As I understand it he don't even wear one. Let him come. We'll bury him out in back of the cabin with the prospector. Then we'll get on with your plan. We can recruit somebody else if you think it's necessary. Your plan is still a good one. I'm not letting any backwoods buffalo hunter spoil it for us.'

That summary made McComb feel

better. With the Iron Kid standing with him there was no way O'Brien could take them down. Since they had no idea where O'Brien was, McComb would wait for him to make his move. They would go about their daily routine between the cabin and the saloon, and wherever O'Brien found them they would confront him and kill him.

Then their futures would be just as rosy as ever.

McComb felt the tension in him dissipate, and a surge of confidence took hold of him that he knew would ensure his survival.

★   ★   ★

O'Brien had gone to a small cafe across from the Occidental and was sitting at a table by himself, eating a beef stew that was a special offering on the menu. When he used his left arm it hurt, but he ignored it.

At a nearby table sat an older

silver-haired man and a ten-year-old-boy who was his grandson. O'Brien didn't notice, but the two looked over toward him regularly and then spoke between themselves in soft tones.

When O'Brien was almost finished with his meal the boy got up from his chair and walked over to O'Brien. O'Brien turned to regard him curiously.

'Are you the buffalo hunter called O'Brien?'

O'Brien looked him over.

'Get away, kid.' He went back to his stew.

'I think you are,' the boy persisted.' And me and my grandpa want to thank you for what you done over at the Occidental.'

O'Brien put his fork down. He swigged a small drink of beer, and set the glass down.

'I didn't do that for you. I did it for me.' He ran a finger through his dark mustache. 'Now you get on. You hear?' His Stetson and rifle were lying on an adjacent chair, within reach. He grabbed the hat and settled it onto dark, long hair.

'OK. But we're proud to meet you, O'Brien. I hope you do the same to their partners out at the cabin.' He started walking away.

'Hold up there a minute,' O'Brien called after him. The boy turned and came back to the table.

'Yes, sir?'

'Do you know where that cabin is?'

The older man had come over behind the boy, and he now answered for him.

'He don't. But I do.'

O'Brien looked him over. 'All right.'

'I seen them there. There in that prospector's cabin south of town about a mile. On the old post road. You can't miss it. And we ain't seen that prospector in town since they moved in out there.'

O'Brien looked at his plate. 'That figures. The old man is dead and buried, if I know McComb.'

'Damn!' the old fellow swore. 'Well,

the law here don't do nothing about nothing. I hope you get out there, young fellow. We've seen what you can do.' He leaned down. 'But listen. He's got that Iron Kid Purvis with him. That boy has won medals for shooting. Before he went bad. Together, they would be almost impossible to kill.'

O'Brien picked up the rifle and sent a little thrill of excitement skittering through the boy.

'You been real helpful,' he said to them. 'Nice talking to you.'

Then he rose and left with them staring after him.

For the next forty-eight hours O'Brien did nothing, figuring that the left arm would be at a definite disadvantage during that time. By the end of the second day the arm felt better and he could use it without substantial restriction. It would have been safer to sleep out on the trail, but he had taken a chance and taken a room at the smaller hotel in town, warning management again about keeping his presence private. It worked.

Meanwhile McComb and Purvis had stayed put for most of the time at the cabin, waiting for O'Brien to appear and discussing ways to ambush him and take his deadly rifle out of play.

In mid-afternoon of that second day after O'Brien's learning where they were, McComb was becoming impatient with the waiting, and angry.

'Damn him!' he spat out to Purvis as they sat together in the cabin. 'Why doesn't he come?'

'Maybe he gave it up and rode out,' Purvis suggested. 'When he found out there's still two fast guns waiting for him out here.'

'He wouldn't do that,' McComb told him.

'Maybe he hasn't figured out where we are yet,' Purvis went on. 'Who knows we're out here?'

McComb rose from the table. 'I'd like to know if he's still in town. Maybe

I'll check at Langley's again. I think that clerk had something to hide. I might just ride in there.'

'You could run into him alone.'

'Not likely. If I do, I'll kill him.' Bitterly he added, 'I'll be back here in less than an hour. If he shows up you can hold him off till I get back.'

'He'll be dead before you get here,' Purvis said easily.

McComb left within five minutes. Within another half-hour O'Brien rode up over a rise of ground and had the cabin in view.

He reined in and studied the cabin. He saw that there was only one horse tied up outside, and it wasn't McComb's mount. If O'Brien went on in, McComb could be waiting in ambush somewhere. Or he could arrive back at the most inopportune time.

He decided to go on in.

He dismounted fifty yards from the cabin, and hitched the appaloosa secluded in a small stand of cottonwoods. Then he walked down to the cabin with the

Winchester at the ready.

Inside, Purvis was so relaxed about the way things were going that he was making himself a hot cup of coffee at a fireplace. When they took over the cabin there had been a long spit-rod over the fire, but there were no hooks to hang a pot on, so Purvis had thrown the rod out into the yard. O'Brien walked over it as he quietly approached the open cabin door, having removed his spurs before he left the appaloosa. He arrived at the doorway without Purvis hearing him.

He levelled the rifle at Purvis, whose back was to him.

'Hold it right there.'

Purvis whirled around, both hands going for his guns.

'I wouldn't,' O'Brien said casually. He didn't want to kill him. He wanted to know where McComb was, and if he was coming back. Purvis dropped his hands to his sides.

'So you're O'Brien.'

'So you're the Iron Kid.'

'That's what some folks call me.'

'You look like a walking armory,' O'Brien said. 'Why don't you get rid of them Wells Fargos?'

Purvis began to understand the seriousness of his situation.

'Look, we can talk about this, can't we?'

'If they ain't on the floor in thirty seconds you'll take their place there.'

Purvis looked down the barrel of the rifle. Then, very reluctantly, he unbuckled his gunbelt and dropped it to the floor.

'Now the shoulder gun,' O'Brien ordered him.

Purvis hesitated, then removed the Joslyn .44 from its holster and carefully laid it on the nearby table.

'What else is there?' O'Brien said.

'Nothing.'

'Turn around.'

Purvis swore under his breath and turned. O'Brien stepped forward and removed the Harrington pocket pistol from his waist. He shook his head. And he threw it onto the table, too.

'Now step away from the table,' O'Brien told him. 'And let's talk about McComb.'

But when Purvis turned back there was desperation in his eyes. O'Brien saw it too late. With the Winchester now hanging loosely under O'Brien's arm, Purvis suddenly hurled himself maniacally at the hunter. He was almost as tall as O'Brien, and his weight as he hit O'Brien drove him back through the doorway the door jamb tore the gun from his grasp. It clattered to the floor.

Both men hit the ground hard outside the cabin. Pain rocketed up O'Brien's left arm. He had been as careless as Purvis for a moment. He still had the skinning knife in a boot, but couldn't get at it. Purvis was pummelling his face with his fists; O'Brien tried to catch them and hold them. The men rolled over and over on the ground, partially rising then falling again, as O'Brien tried to get this suddenly wild man under control. The tethered mounts were rearing and plunging. Eventually O'Brien got his feet under him. Savagely he hauled Purvis up and threw a rock-hammer punch into his face, breaking his nose in two places. O'Brien's left arm was screaming at him.

In the moment it took for O'Brien to get a breath into him Purvis scrambled to his feet drunkenly, blood running down his face. He ran, staggering, back to the cabin, and fell heavily against the wall there, just beside the doorway. A twisted grin came over his bloody face.

'You lose, hunter!' he said breathlessly. 'All the guns are inside, and I'm between you and them. Too bad! You're dead!'

But O'Brien had picked up the long spit-bar, which was at his feet, while Purvis was running to the cabin. One end of it was unfinished and rather jagged. As Purvis was finishing his tirade, standing at the cabin door, O'Brien hurled the makeshift spear at him violently.

The rod hurtled through the air like a

striking rattlesnake and plunged into Purvis's mid-chest. His eyes widened as it penetrated completely through him, nailing him to the cabin wall behind him.

He looked down at the rod incredulously, then grabbed it with both hands. He cast one more look at O'Brien, then he hung there, lifeless.

O'Brien walked tiredly over to him. He touched the rod; there was no vibration on it. O'Brien grunted.

'What good did all them guns do you, Kid?'

He leaned against the wall beside the corpse. He was hurting worse than maybe he ever had. He was so tired he felt like lying down on the soft bed back at the hotel and just forgetting McComb for a day or two. But he couldn't do that now. It was McComb he had come after, and he didn't know what McComb would do if he found Purvis.

He had no choice. He had to ride into town and look for him.

O'Brien stopped at the Langley boarding house first. There was nobody at the registration area, but when O'Brien called out the clerk whom he and McComb had dealt with before came out from a back room.

'Oh. You.'

'Yes, me.'

'I could have been killed because of you, mister. That McComb threatened me.'

'Has he been back?'

'He was here not long before you. Asking about you again.'

'And?'

'And I kept my mouth shut. I didn't want to be the cause of your early demise. That boy looks pretty dangerous, and my guess is he wants to kill you.'

'You might say it's mutual,' O'Brien muttered. 'How long ago did he leave?'

'Maybe half-hour.'

'Did he say where he was headed?'

'No. But I saw him ride off toward the Occidental. He mumbled something as he left. About not waiting anymore.'

O'Brien nodded to himself. 'Well. Appreciate the help.'

'What are you going to do?'

'I'm going to kill him,' O'Brien said simply. Then he turned and left.

O'Brien rode on down to the Occidental saloon. As he approached, he saw a crowd of men standing outside the place, near the doorway. He frowned slightly and dismounted, wrapping the appaloosa's reins over a long hitching post. He slid the retrieved Winchester from its saddle scabbard, levered a cartridge into its chamber and mounted the steps to the doors.

'You going in with that?' a young cowpoke accosted him.

'So what?' O'Brien growled.

The cowboy shrugged. 'They might not let you stay. After what happened.'

O'Brien frowned slightly. He took a firm grip on the rifle and pushed through the swing doors.

Just inside, he stopped frozen in place by what he saw.

There were two bodies lying in awkward positions on the floor, not far away. One of the dead men was a lawman with a badge still stuck to a blood stained shirt.

The other was Cyrus McComb.

O'Brien stared hard, not moving. A rancher was kneeling over the lawman, shaking his head.

'No need for a doc. They're both dead.'

O'Brien's head was spinning. After this long journey to arrive at this point, reality was unacceptable. He walked to where McComb lay and stood over him.

'Are you sure about this one?' he said to the kneeling man. The fellow rose, and nodded.

'Got one right through the spine. It was a wild shoot-out.'

O'Brien shook his head, still trying to absorb this unbelievable information.

'Who's the lawman?'

'Oh, he's a federal marshal who was after McComb for that bank hold-up east of here. Seems somebody recognized McComb's voice from when he used to live here. The marshal tried to arrest him and McComb went crazy. They both just started shooting. A bystander got hit; he's down at the doctor.'

'Good God!' O'Brien mumbled.

'He came in looking for you,' the barkeep called out. The rancher looked at the rifle under O'Brien's arm.

'That makes sense,' he said to himself. O'Brien glanced over at him.

'As he was taking his last breaths, he mumbled, 'Too bad, hunter.'' The rancher caught O'Brien's eye. 'Was there something between you two?'

O'Brien grunted. 'A little something.'

'He killed two of McComb's no-good partners,' the bartender called out again.

The rancher's gaze fixed on O'Brien, and every eye in the saloon focused on him.

'You came here to kill him,' said the rancher. 'And the law beat you to it.'

O'Brien met his look, but said nothing. With one last look at McComb's lifeless body he turned and left the saloon.

Outside the crowd was dispersing. O'Brien walked down to the appaloosa and leaned on its flank. He felt as if he had been punched in the midriff. He turned to the horse.

'It's over,' he said quietly.

He felt different. He wasn't tired any more. His left arm didn't hurt, either. It was as if McComb's death had released some healing force in him, and he felt, at least for now, that he might never again feel as bad as he had out at the cabin.

He slid the Winchester back into its scabbard and patted the appaloosa's rump. He was ready to leave Billings for good.

He took the reins off the hitch rail and mounted the horse. All around him was the bustle and noise of the town. It grated on his ears.

'I hear there's a big herd down south of here a couple days' ride,' he said softly to the animal. 'A wide dark carpet on the prairie just waiting to be culled. Where the grass is shoulder high and the air is sweet as honey.' He gazed off into the distance.

'Let's go have us a look.'

Then he rode off into his newly created world.

We do hope that you have enjoyed reading this large print book.

Did you know that all of our titles are available for purchase?

We publish a wide range of high quality large print books including:
Romances, Mysteries, Classics
General Fiction
Non Fiction and Westerns

Special interest titles available in large print are:
The Little Oxford Dictionary
Music Book, Song Book
Hymn Book, Service Book

Also available from us courtesy of Oxford University Press:
Young Readers' Dictionary
(large print edition)
Young Readers' Thesaurus
(large print edition)

For further information or a free brochure, please contact us at:
Ulverscroft Large Print Books Ltd.,
The Green, Bradgate Road, Anstey,
Leicester, LE7 7FU, England.
Tel: (00 44) **0116 236 4325**
Fax: (00 44) **0116 234 0205**

NOLAN'S LAW

Lee Lejeune

After his mother and father die, and the girl he hopes to marry turns him down, Jude James decides to abandon his rented homestead and ride for the West along with Josh, a young exslave seeking sanctuary. Eventually they fall in with a gang led by Brod Nolan, who claims to rob the rich to feed the poor. But there is more to this than meets the eye — and the two friends find themselves embroiled in a series of bloodcurdling encounters in which they must kill or be killed . . .

PIRATES OF THE DESERT

C. J. Sommers

The locals call the sand dunes of the Arizona Territory southland a white ocean. One man, Barney Shivers, carries the comparison a little further when he orders his men to attack any freight shipping that he does not control, and steal the goods on board. A little old lady, Lolly Amos, contracts her nephew, Captain Parthenon Downs of the Arizona rangers, to fight back. Downs eagerly takes on the challenge — but little does he realize that his decision will draw him into a war against two bands of pirates . . .

THE VIGILANCE MAN

Fenton Sadler

For twelve-year-old Brent Cutler, seeing his father lynched was the most powerful influence on his young life, giving him an abiding and lifelong hatred of injustice in any form. As an adult, he returns to the town where he grew up, as a representative of the District Attorney's office — and finds himself going head to head with the man responsible for the death of his father a decade earlier. There will be hard words and tough actions before Cutler can finally lay the demons of his childhood to rest.

BAD DEAL IN BUCKSKIN

Ethan Flagg

Two unemployed wranglers are given a gold nugget for helping an old prospector named Huggy Johnson when his wagon breaks down. Alamo Todd Heffridge and his partner Kid Streater unwittingly sell the nugget to an unscrupulous assay agent in the Arizona town of Buckskin. When Huggy is shot dead over a map that pin-points the location of the infamous Lost Dutchman Mine, the two wranglers are accused of the crime and arrested. Can they escape from jail and find the real killers?

TERROR IN TOMBSTONE

Paul Bedford

Former lawman Rance Toller and his lover Angie Sutter foil a stagecoach robbery just outside the frontier settlement of Tombstone, Arizona, and in the process capture the notorious gunfighter Johnny Ringo. As a result, Rance is persuaded to accept the vacant position of town marshal. Unfortunately, he soon falls foul of the Grand Central mining operators, led by E. B. Gage, who want the law on their terms. With the dubious help of his new friend, Doc Holliday, Rance has to fight for his life against Gage's ruthless enforcers . . .